Crime In Passion

Stacey Haynes

Stacey Haynes

Copyright © 2020 Stacey Haynes

All rights reserved.

ISBN: 9798611343685

DEDICATIONS

Dedication from Stacey Haynes

I'd like to dedicate this book to all who enjoy romance and adventure. This is my first book, with only my name on it, and I am so thankful for everyone who encouraged me to do this.

I'd like to thank my family for helping me through certain scenes in this book. My family is my biggest support group!

I also would like to thank all the readers for their comments and encouragement. You, as well, inspire me to keep entertaining. Your comments make me feel more confident in my writing. THANK YOU!

Thanks to my BETA team for helping me find the errors, and for the encouraging words you gave me after reading this story. You are all awesome!

Special Thanks

Special thanks to Teresa Pearson and Veronica Mesia for editing this book for me. I'm terrible at grammar and commas and they are outstanding in this field.

Another big Thanks goes to my sister, Marie Higgins, as she has helped me through this new book publishing process.

Also, special thanks to my cover designer: Got You Covered. Lisa did an amazing job on the cover.

Prologue

Puffs of smoke billowed from the overturned armored truck that was resting in a ditch. Lying in a pool of blood in the ground was a man, dressed in black. The truck's back doors were blown off. Inside the not-so-secured back area, one guard lay dead from a gunshot wound to the lower abdomen as well as a shot to the neck. The passenger guard in front was also dead with a shot to the head. The driver, barely conscious reached for his cell phone.

Dialing 911 and in a faint voice he whispered, "We've been robbed."

Earlier in the week, a rare, blue diamond necklace was flown in from England, The Midnight Star. This diamond was put on display at the Johnson Towers Museum and now was being transported back to the airport in an armored truck. The diamond was carefully placed in a large security lockbox and handed off to the four armed men who occupied the security vehicle. The men sat in standard procedure while transporting important items; two in the back and two in the front. What started out as a secure pickup from the museum in Marriott, suddenly turned completely deadly.

Justin Doxy was one of the men who sat in the back. He kept his eyes on the lockbox. Sitting in the back of the truck was not the smoothest of rides. Every corner that was taken would move him in his seat. The other guard sat looking at his phone; playing a game. Justin took a quick glance at this watch. He sucked a deep breath in.

"Wanna play?" Justin asked the other man.

He looked up with a confused look but then his eyes went as large as plums as Justin's fist went flying into the guy's face. Justin pushed the rifle away from the guard as he continued throwing punches at him. They bounced against the insides of the back of the truck as they took turns being tossed about in the fight. Their movements were shaking the truck.

The driver began feeling some sharp movements that rocked the back of the truck, shaking it enough to cause concern. The guard in the passenger seat pulled out the radio and called to the back.

"What's going on back there?"

No one answered. The passenger turned to open the little window that gave a peek hole to the rear. Just as his hands touched the slider to open the window a popping sound came from the back.

"Someone's been shot!" the guard yelled to the driver. "Pull over."

The driver maneuvered the vehicle to the side of the road and brought it to a stop. The guard opened the window just as another popping noise pushed him back towards the dashboard, bullet to the head from someone in the back.

The driver frantically reached for his phone to call for help. From out of nowhere, a huge dump truck plowed into the parked armored truck, clipping the right rear quarter panel sending it into a half-spin. The driver fell forward against the steering wheel. The dump truck continued pushing the armored truck sending it tumbling into a ditch.

From the back, Justin cursed as he searched for the lockbox. He found it tucked under the bench where the other guard lay bleeding out. Justin had shot him, in the abdomen, just under the bullet proof vest, right before the truck stopped. The man wasn't dead yet, but he was losing consciousness quickly.

Justin rushed to the back door and tried desperately to get out. A separate radio on the man's pants came alive as a voice echoed over it.

"Justin, back away from the door."

Justin cursed. "Victor, you didn't stick to the plan!"

"Move away!" Victor's voice boomed over the radio.

Justin rushed to the far end of the truck just as a loud bang echoed in his ears. Smoked filled the truck. Justin grabbed the lockbox and jumped out of the truck. Another man was there, dressed in black, tucking C-4 into his duffle bag.

"Victor, you were too early," Justin yelled at him.

"We can discuss this later. Let's go!" Victor grabbed his bag and began his climb up to the street where a black Rolls Royce had pulled up.

Standing guard at the car was a woman, also dressed in black, with a ski mask on. Her slim frame held a large semi-automatic rifle. She scanned the roads looking for anyone that could ruin the heist. Inside the car, a man sat behind the wheel, tapping impatiently on the steering wheel.

Justin took a few steps following Victor before collapsing to the ground as a sharp report of a gunshot rang through the air.

"Justin!" The female voice yelled as she began firing her own rifle towards the armored truck, hitting the already injured guard from the back of the truck, killing him.

Victor dropped to the ground and crawled over to Justin who lay dead on the ground from a shot to the head. Victor grabbed the lockbox, took one last look at Justin then turned away hurrying up to the car.

"Victor, you cannot leave him," the woman's voice cried out.

"Go. He's dead. We got what we came for," Victor said climbing into the front seat.

The woman quickly got in the car.

"Go, Bruce." Victor pounded the dashboard.

"You didn't give him enough time," the woman yelled at Victor. "That was not a part of our plan. You changed the plan at the last minute by pushing the truck too soon. Justin could still be alive. You killed him."

"Constance." Victor glared towards her. "We all knew the consequences in doing this job. Justin should have ensured they were dead before leaving the truck."

"Is that diamond worth all this?" Bruce, the driver, asked.

"Oh, yes." Victor opened the box, brushing his fingers across the diamond's blue sparkling surface. "Around the perfect neck, it will fetch the greatest fortune of my career."

ONE

Jessica Cook wore her professional smile as she assisted the customer who was next in her line at the bank. Across the counter, a small silver-haired lady pushed a huge Mason jar full of pennies in front of her. Jessica peered over the jar and the little lady smiled sweetly up at her, politely asking her to count her money. *Seriously?* She glanced up at the clock hanging on the wall and saw that the hour hand was very close to the six. She sighed softly as she slid her dark rimmed glasses up on her nose and lifted the big jar off the counter and headed back to the coin sorter.

Her eyes roamed around the bank and focused on Trent Hawkins, one of the other tellers. She remembered him from high school, though seven years ago, how could she ever forget him? His blonde hair and tall, muscular frame made any girl swoon as he walked by. He used to be on the basketball team, so she wasn't the only one who had a major crush on him. However, there was no way he would've noticed her. She hadn't been popular. In fact, not many people knew she existed. Her focus had been on being more studious than social. Her only claim to fame was that her father was on the city council, and then two years after graduating high school, her father became the newly-appointed mayor.

Now, Trent was a teller at Winslow Bank with her. His father was the bank manager; so of course, he'd hire his son to work there. But luckily for her, she still got to gaze at him when his back was turned. Trent had matured over seven years, and, deep inside she really wanted him to notice her.

To Jessica's dismay, Trent was always flirting with Demi, the bleached blonde beauty with the pearly white teeth, while in the drive-thru window area. Demi kept touching his arm and laughing as they worked. It made Jessica sick to her stomach to watch this. Trent glanced back over his shoulder and his eyes met up with Jessica's. She quickly looked away and ran right into the coin sorter machine and started to drop the jar she was holding. Though her hold on the jar was firm, the pennies spilled out onto the floor making clinking noises on the tile.

"Oh, no!" Jessica cried out as she quickly stooped to the floor to start gathering all the pennies, her face burning.

Immediately, Charlene, another teller, came running over to her to help her pick them up.

"I-I can't believe I did that," Jessica stammered from her nervousness.

"If you weren't ogling Trent, then maybe you wouldn't have dropped it," Charlene teased in a whisper.

"Does everyone know I watch him?" Jessica's cheeks flushed further.

"You just need to go talk to him." Charlene picked up a handful of pennies and tossed them back into the jar Jessica still held.

"Goodness, no!" she gasped and put the jar on the floor before she dropped it again. "I can't talk to him. He'd know I like him."

"Well, yeah. That's the whole point, isn't it?"

Jessica nervously twisted her long curly brown hair that was hanging to the side over her shoulder. She hated how thick and wavy her hair was. No matter how hard she tried to blow dry it straight, it would always frizz up. She usually pulled it back somehow in a pony-tail or bun so it didn't look too crazy.

She pushed her dark rimmed glasses back up on her nose again and stood up with the jar of pennies. Hopefully they got all of them. She tossed a quick look back to the drive thru booth. Trent and Demi were laughing at something, probably her clumsiness. Jessica turned on the coin sorter and tossed the pennies inside for the machine to sort and count. She stared longingly at her reflection in the polished side panel of the coin sorter. Trent probably thought she was unattractive because of her glasses. She had considered switching to contacts, but was just too scared to stick her fingers in her eyes. No, glasses would just have to do.

The machine beeped, signaling that the coin count was completed. Jessica took the receipt back to the silver haired lady.

"Do you want this in your account or in cash?" Jessica asked politely, looking over the counter again.

"My account please," the old woman replied.

"Do you have your account card?"

"Oh, I have it in here somewhere." The woman proceeded to pull out almost every piece of candy, used tissues, coins, and pens out of her purse before she found her wallet.

Jessica rolled her eyes. She really was thankful for this job, but it was these slow people that irritated her.

The woman slid a laminated card to her. "Oh, here it is."

Jessica quickly entered in the numbers and handed the card back to the woman while she slowly returned all her junk back to her purse. The money was quickly added to the account and she printed out a receipt.

"Anything else I can help you with?" Jessica sure hoped she would say no because it was now two minutes past six o'clock.

"No, I believe that is all. Thank you dear." The old woman strolled slowly out the door.

Jessica closed the doors at her window and began the count for the end of the day. She had to hurry since her parents had invited her to come to their place, the mayor's mansion, for the city council meeting. Jessica was not into politics, in fact, they bored her, but her mother had personally invited her to listen in.

The council meetings always had a light dinner before-hand and the city talk afterwards. This was one thing that made her father popular. He had been a wonderful mayor thus far and had done a lot of good for Winslow City, and in turn, the people adored him.

Jessica pulled up to her parents' home. She lived in the mansion for a few years until she found herself a studio apartment near the college campus. Being on her own proved she could handle any challenge that came her way.

She quietly entered in the front door and could hear the clanking of forks on plates as guests ate their dinner. It was nearing the end of the meal and she didn't want to make a grand entrance. She found a seat in the back of the meeting room and pulled out her romance novel and picked up where she left off; where her hero, Austin, was about to reveal his true identity to the heroine, Ellen, that he was a spy. Inside a book was where Jessica found her romance. No one could be better than the heroes in her books. They were always so handsome, strong, and brave.

When the meeting began, she tried to pay attention as they talked about the potholes on the main street, the budget, and then some people wanting an afternoon program at the library for kids. Her book was more interesting than these issues. Finally, the last topic of discussion was some recent burglaries in their town as well as in the neighboring towns, and this caught Jessica's attention.

"The police department is working these cases," Mayor Cook said to the crowd. "But remember, if anyone sees anything, please contact the police department and let them do their job."

"Will police be patrolling the streets more often?" A citizen asked.

"I'm sure they will have every available officer watching out for our town," the Mayor announced.

"What about the Winslow Bank? Is that safe?" Someone else inquired.

Jessica sat ram-rod straight as fear snaked into her body. She'd heard of convenient stores being robbed, but never the big banks. Only in movies were the big banks targeted. The robbers would have to be stupid to step foot into a highly secured building.

"Winslow Bank has all the up to date security features, so I wouldn't worry too much," Mayor Cook reassured. "Just keep an eye out for suspicious activities and make sure you let the authorities know if you see anything. Don't try to be the hero, just report them."

When the meeting adjourned, Jessica joined her parents in the family room while the staff cleaned up the home.

"We're so happy you made it." Mayor Cook gave her a kiss on the cheek.

"I almost didn't. A customer was being a bit on the slow side."

A picture of a huge diamond that was on the front page of a newspaper caught her eye and she picked it up. Jessica couldn't believe the newspaper was still reporting on the stolen diamond that happened almost a year ago. The Midnight Star was a royal blue diamond brought over from England to be on display at an art exhibit in the neighboring town. The diamond's worth was around three million dollars. The best security was to be in place, yet the diamond ended up being stolen.

"Was this group of thieves the same ones that stole the diamond in Marriot?" she asked.

"Sadly, I'm sure those people are long gone and these other crimes that are happening around town are being committed by another group. I'm just speculating, though." Her father loosened his tie.

"You be extra careful, sweetie." Mrs. Cook took a hold of Jessica's hands. "Banks are usually targeted for burglary."

"Don't scare her, Donna," her father said. "These kinds of people don't do things in broad daylight, and they never take hostages or kill anyone. They are professional thieves and they know how to get in and out without being noticed."

"Well, that makes me feel better," Jessica lied. Deep down, she was terrified of being robbed at the bank now. "Anyway, I've got to get back home. I have training material I still need to read up on for a new program they installed at work." She walked over and hugged her parents. "I'll be safe, don't worry."

Even if she reassured her parents that she was safe, as Jessica drove back to her apartment, she kept her eyes open for any type of suspicious activity that could be happening around town. All the talk of crime made her paranoid and more aware of everything going on around her. Before she turned onto her street, a cyclist passed by, making her jump. This was exactly why she never went to those meetings. She even, long ago, stopped watching the evening news because every problem that was brought up made her depressed and fearful.

She checked her front door multiple times throughout the night to ensure the bolts were locked. It was now she wished the landlord would allow her to have a pet. At least a dog would notify her of any strangers approaching. She really should chill out; these people were only after expensive stuff, none of which she had in her measly little apartment.

Jessica curled up with her book and a cup of hot chocolate and read her hunk of a hero in her romance story. He was a sexy super spy who wined and dined the women he encountered. Besides taking the heroine in her book on adventures, he was a romantic man which left her breathless as she read about him. She wished she could have these types of adventures with a man. Heck, she wished this type of man even existed. Even though she loved her novels, she always felt sad when she had to face reality because she wasn't dating anyone right now, and that was what upset her.

Her last boyfriend only lasted a few weeks. There was only one reason she could think of as why it didn't last long; she was too shy. Guys don't like shy girls. They want outgoing and spontaneous women, traits she did not have, but the women in her novels did. She loved to read so she could hide away and pretend that she was a spontaneous heroine and would be rescued by her hero. Such a wonderful romantic moment it would be. If only Trent would notice her and be her hero. She always imagined his strong arms around her every night as she drifted off to sleep, and tonight wouldn't be any different.

Saturday morning didn't turn out the way she wanted it to. In addition to her oversleeping this morning, problems on her old Chevy Classic model car started to rear their ugly heads. It took her multiple times to get the car to even start running on its own. She had some money in savings, but when it came to cars, those types of fixes would probably drain her account.

Jessica didn't want to take out a loan, but that was the more adult thing to do than asking her father for money. Besides, she wanted to prove she could be independent.

At work, it was as busy as it ever was. Jessica looked for suspicious faces as she studied every person as they came into the bank. So far, everyone was just the normal Winslow City citizens. Good, more time to watch Trent.

"Jessica," Charlene whispered over the wall during a small break.

Jessica looked up and moved closer to the wall while she stacked forms on her desk.

"What?"

"Why don't you go talk to him?"

"Who?" Jessica looked around.

"Trent." Charlene motioned with her head towards the drive-thru where he and Demi sat.

"I can't do it." Jessica shook her head.

"You've been watching him a lot today. Go ask him to go with you to a movie or something."

"Charlene, there is no way I can do something like that. He doesn't even know I exist. He never did in high school so why should he now?"

"How are you going to find a guy if you never talk to one?" Charlene asked.

Charlene already had a boyfriend, so she didn't have to worry about being alone on Friday and Saturday nights. The thought of going to a movie with Trent would be wonderful, but there was no way she could bring herself to ask him.

Jessica shook her head again. "I don't know. I guess I'm old fashioned. I want him to come to me. You know, give me a rose and tell me I'm the only one for him."

"They don't make those types of guys anymore." Charlene dusted off her counter. "I'd love to go on a double date with you, but you need to find a guy. Maybe we can set you up with someone."

"No. That'll make me look desperate."

"I don't think so." Charlene was a good sport. She had tried.

At the end of the day, Jessica sat in her car as she watched Trent and Demi laughing together by Demi's car. Why couldn't she be more like her? She needed more confidence in herself. She was pretty, she just needed someone to tell that to her more often.

She jabbed the key in the ignition and turned the car to the starting position. The car rumbled and stopped. Taking in a calming breath, she tried it again. It did the same thing.

"Come on, baby," Jessica coaxed the car. "I promise I will take you to the mechanic's on Monday."

She turned the key a few more times and finally, on the fifth try, it started up. The car shook but at least it was running. Jessica quickly put the car in gear and headed towards the grocery store to pick up dinner.

All down the street, the car sputtered and shook as if it was going to die at any second. She figured if she moved off the main road through town, she wouldn't be too embarrassed if the car did stall completely at a stop light. Before her car would stop completely, she turned to the back streets.

Less traffic and not as many stop lights was another good reason to be on this road. Even though it took a bit longer to get to the store, it was well worth it. Jessica stopped at the stop sign and looked both ways. When the intersection was clear, the inevitable happened, she put her foot on the gas pedal and the car hesitated then stalled completely.

"No, no, no," Jessica moaned. "You cannot do this to me. Please car--please start."

She coasted the car to the further right curb and put it in park. Jessica tried to start the car up again, but nothing happened. She smacked her hands on the steering wheel and then pulled the hood release. When she opened the car door, she figured that the only way to rid her of frustration would be to slam it shut. Sure, it did make her feel a tiny bit better, but it didn't fix the car.

Peering under the hood, she tried to think of what guys look for when they are in this position. She pulled the dipstick out and could see there was oil on it; that was good. She looked at the battery cables to make sure they were connected.

"Oh," Jessica waved her hand across the engine, "this is hopeless. You – stupid – car!"

She knew her parents were in some civic type meetings this afternoon and she really didn't want to bother them, but there was no other way. Her dad would know what to do. Jessica closed the hood of the car and reached for the door handle to open it. As she did, the door remained closed.

"No!" Jessica groaned aloud as she placed her head on the window as she peered inside. She saw her keys in the car, along with her purse and cell phone. She slightly remembered hearing a click as she slammed her door, but she didn't look to see what it was. Apparently, it was the doors locking.

She kicked the tire of the car before she began walking in the direction of the store. The afternoon weather was not bad for early September, so the walk was pleasant, but long. Maybe the walk would ease her stress of the car. There was a short cut that would shorten the walking time by a good ten minutes. The alley ran along the backside of the strip mall that was just off the main street. Usually delivery trucks took this road to bypass the busier main road thru Winslow.

Down the alley were back doors that led into the different stores of the strip mall. There was an income tax preparation store, a pawn shop, a small jewelry store, and a medical supply store. A white cleaning van was parked in the alley.

Walking alone in an alley sent chills up her spine. Jessica quickened her pace. Winslow was a clean town so not many drunks or thugs would be out scaring people at this time of day.

As she reached the back end of the cleaning van, her quickened pace was brought to a halt as the back door to the jewelry store flung open and out rushed three people dressed in white jumpsuits. Jessica's feet stopped and her mouth gaped open. Fear seeped further into her veins.

They each were carrying duffle bags and two of them wore black ski masks. The third person had already pulled the mask off revealing the face of a woman. Their surprised faces matched hers. Should she scream? Panic rose in her chest but instead of screaming, she turned to get out of there as fast as she could.

"Get her!" the woman without the mask yelled.

Jessica heard the van doors open and the engine start up. But it was the arms that quickly grabbed her that scared her the most. One of the men in the white jumpsuit grabbed her around the waist and began dragging her back.

"Let me go!" Jessica screamed and started to kick with her feet. Her glasses fell off her face as the man pushed her inside of the van. Jessica continued screaming to draw as much attention as she could to them. The woman who was with them ripped off a long piece of duct tape and placed it over her mouth then tossed the roll to the guy who grabbed her and began wrapping her wrists and then feet with the tape. Jessica kicked the guy multiple times still trying to get away.

"Jack, drive!" the man with the duct tape yelled. The van was put into motion and back out on the main road.

"I'm sorry to do this," the woman said as she brought up her hand holding a gun and proceeded to whack Jessica on the head with the butt of the gun.

Bright lights entered her eyes and she fell backwards into the woman. Blackness started moving in her eyesight and it seemed she was heading into a dark tunnel. Her head was aching really badly and then she closed her eyes. A man's voice sounded like it was being spoken through a long tube.

"We could have left her, you know."

"She saw my face," the woman said.

Jessica blacked out completely.

TWO

The meeting was finally winding down. Sean Turpin looked at his watch. 8:30 p.m. It was a two-hour drive to get home. He stood up from his seat and stretched his arms behind his head extending his six-foot frame an inch or two taller. These seminars always ran a bit later when there was mingling. Sean didn't want to do that tonight, even though Monica, the young gal from Dawson Safe, kept smiling at him. It would be nice to make some conversation with her. However, his mind kept wondering when his phone was going to ring to alert him of the evening's job that took place without him. No time for talking with beautiful ladies because as soon as he did, he knew his phone would ring.

Sean gathered up his folders and placed them in his briefcase. He loosened his tie. Monica slinked over to him brushing her blond hair away from her face.

"So, did you learn a lot?" she batted her eyes at him.

"As much as I need to know." Sean smiled casually at her. "Have you worked with Dawson Safe long?"

"Three years. This was my first conference. How about you? What company do you work for?"

"Turpin Security; I'm the owner." He smiled as he raised his eyebrows at her.

"I've heard of you then." She scooted in a bit closer. "I think you have been taking people away from us." She winked.

"Possibly." Exactly as he predicted, his phone vibrated in his pocket. "Excuse me while I get this."

Sean stepped back from Monica. He opened his flip phone to answer while he walked away.

"It's about time," Sean's voice turned stern. "Victor is waiting for an answer. Any problems?"

"Umm," Bruce began. "Yes, there was one problem."

"It was a simple job." Sean shook his head while on the phone. "How can there be a problem?"

"Yes, it was a simple job," Bruce agreed. "We cleaned it out. No issues there."

"Then what is the problem?"

"It's Connie," Bruce blamed. "She freaked out and well…"

"Spit it out, Bruce." Sean was growing impatient as he brushed his fingers over his short well- groomed beard.

"We have a witness."

"What are you talking about?" Sean asked as he paced in the back of the conference room.

"We came out and there was a girl who was in the alley. She saw us. She screamed. Connie said to grab her."

"You what?" He quickly walked to the far corner and lowered his voice. "You kidnapped a girl?"

"Blame it on Connie."

Sean cussed multiple times then blew out a stressful sigh. "I'm coming home. You had better figure out what to do with her by the time I get there."

Sean closed the phone as he wandered back to the table. Why in the world would Connie grab a witness? They knew better. This was not going to not make Victor pleased. Sean had worked with Victor for almost a year and he knew Victor did not kidnap people. Now he was going to have to explain this to Victor. Or, maybe he should just have Bruce explain it to him.

"Flip phone." Monica pointed as Sean put his phone back in his pocket. "Nice."

"Well, you should know they have better security than a smart phone."

"You didn't look too happy with that call," she observed. "Everything alright?"

Sean picked up his briefcase that was on the chair where he was sitting.

"My partners messed up a job," Sean explained. "Now I have to go fix it. It's the downfalls of being the owner of the business."

"I'm sorry to hear that," Monica said. "Well, have a good evening and drive carefully."

"I suppose we can talk more at the next conference in a few months. You will be there, right?" Sean asked putting on the charm.

"As long as my boss agrees to let me go." She stretched her hand out and Sean took it in his. "I hope to visit longer, maybe over drinks."

Sean held her soft hand for a moment, nodded then released it. He did wish he had more time to visit. Once he was seated in his silver Camaro, he pulled his tie off completely and prayed the cops would not be out tonight. He needed to get home quickly to get this problem fixed. With a hostage to get rid of, this will now slow his plans down.

****

Jessica's head throbbed. She blinked her eyes open, but the room was dark and there was nothing to see; to top things off, she had lost her glasses in the struggle. She briefly remembered being brought into this room and placed on the floor. She had been lying on the cold floor drifting in and out of consciousness for who knows how long. When she was asleep, it kept her head from hurting. The duct tape was still over her mouth. Her hands and feet were bound with duct tape. Anxiety was starting to make her squirm. She had to get out of this.

Tears filled her eyes as she tried to sit up. Her head pounded harder. *What was going on? This couldn't be right? I thought these robbers didn't take hostages. Maybe these are different robbers?* Jessica's mind flooded with questions. From beneath the door a sliver of light shone through allowing something to look at. Jessica slowly scooted towards the door. She had no idea what time it was. Did anyone know she was missing? She put her ear up against the door hoping to hear any sound of life. From the distance the sound of a sports reporter on a television spoke giving a description of the football play that just happened. She wasn't alone.

Should she make a noise? Would they hurt her if she did? Jessica's arms tingled from the lack of blood to them from being bound up behind her. She needed to take this risk. With her feet she sent a good hard kick to the door. She kept this up for a few more times. Heavy footsteps stomped up to the door and a hand pounded on the door. Jessica jumped.

"Be quiet in there!" A gruff voice yelled.

She stopped kicking and started to sob again.

"She's probably scared to death," a female voice said. She didn't sound too mean.

"Not my problem," the gruff voice continued. "You are the one who said to grab her."

"I wasn't thinking. She saw us and we needed to do something quick," the woman said. "Sean will know what to do."

"I tell you what *they* are going to do; Sean and Victor are going to kill you for doing this; and maybe her too." The man warned.

"She probably needs to go to the bathroom," the woman said again not fazed by the death sentence that the man suggested. "It has been hours since we took her."

"Hide your face." The heavy footsteps moved away from the door.

Jessica scooted back. Panic filled her body as she kept hearing the words of the man saying she could possibly die. When the door opened a bright light came inside. Jessica squinted and the shape of a woman entered. She had something dark in her hand. Jessica couldn't quite tell what it was until she stepped closer to her. It was a blindfold. As the woman reached for Jessica, she moved back away from her and whimpered. The woman pulled a pocket knife from her pants pocket and flipped it up. Jessica's eyes went wide and tried to scoot back further but she was already up against something metal and cold. The lady sliced the duct tape off of Jessica's feet then replaced the knife in her pocket.

"I'm taking you to the bathroom," the woman told Jessica as she pulled her to her feet. "Don't try anything stupid."

The blindfold was placed over her eyes. Jessica's legs felt wobbly as if she was a newborn fawn. A tug on Jessica's arm brought her feet to shuffling slowly across the room. She really wished she had her hands free so she could feel her way through the darkness. The temperature in the room changed as she moved to the next room. The woman made sure she didn't bump into anything as they walked.

"I'm going to undo your hands, but don't do something you will regret later," the woman warned. "I do have a gun and will shoot you. Do you understand?"

Jessica nodded in between sobs.

"We are in the bathroom. You go and then I take you back," she instructed.

Jessica nodded again. She unbound her hands as promised. Jessica rubbed them quickly to move the circulation through them and then with the blindfold still over her eyes the woman backed Jessica up to a toilet. Jessica felt around to find the seat and then fumbled with her pants and then quickly sat down. This was extremely awkward. Jessica emptied her bladder and stood up and pulled up her pants. The woman led her to the sink to wash up. The tape over her mouth was starting to itch. She fought the urge to pull off the tape.

A soft towel covered her hands and Jessica wiped them dry. She heard the toilet flush and then another tug on Jessica's arm made her walk again. Jessica counted the steps, so she knew where she was going, just in case she needed to make a run for it. Her body wouldn't stop shivering from fear. More tears gathered in her eyes. She didn't want to be locked back in this room. The sound of more tape being unraveled made her sob some more. Her arms were bound again. The woman didn't bind her legs this time.

"Sorry about this," she said. "We just couldn't have any witnesses."

Jessica shook her head and tried to mumble something like, "I wouldn't have told."

"I'd take the tape off your mouth but then you would scream, and well, we can't have that. I don't want to have to knock you out again, so just hang tight until we can figure out what to do with you," she said. She took the blind fold off of Jessica's eyes and left the light on as she stepped out.

Jessica could see something was in the woman's hand, so she wasn't lying, she did have a gun. The door closed and the sound of it locking sent more chills over her body. She slid down carefully to the floor again.

Jessica gazed around the room now that her eyes were focusing a little better, despite the fact she had no glasses on. She was in some type of large utility room. Brooms, mops and buckets were in the room as well as cleaning supplies and paper towels. A washer and dryer were stacked in the corner where she sat earlier. Her bottom was hurting from being on the cold floor.

An odd chattering noise seemed very close to her. She quickly scanned the room to see what it was, hoping it wasn't some rodent. She held her breath as she studied each corner carefully. The chattering stopped. When she turned her head, the sound occurred again. Then it dawned on her, it was her teeth that were chattering. She shook her head from embarrassment.

The pounding in her head would not stop. She wasn't sure if it was better with the lights on or off. Every time she shivered, or her teeth chattered, her head throbbed. She was sure the spot on her head was swelling from the whack the woman gave her. She probably had a concussion and it was probably not good that she had been asleep for a bit.

I don't want to die! Thoughts raced into her head. Jessica tried to think of some happy thoughts so she wouldn't just sit there and cry. The thought of Trent coming to rescue her would for sure make her happy. He would fight those who held her captive and punch them out. She would fall into his arms and he would hold her, kiss her, and protect her, but sadly, no one knew where she was.

Her thoughts of her knight in shining armor coming to the rescue were shattered by a door opening and slamming right next to the room where she was locked in. Jessica jumped and scooted herself more in a corner, shivering from fear. The utility room must be by a back door.

"Bruce! What were you thinking?"

She heard the new deep voice of a man as he passed the room she was shivering in. He didn't sound happy at all as curse words were being tossed about.

"She said to grab her," Jessica heard the other man, who must be Bruce, say. "I wanted to leave her. We could have just knocked her out and left her there."

"Don't look at me," the female said. "I didn't know what to do; she would be able to tell something to the police."

"And now she won't?" The new angry voice was saying. He cursed again. "We are not kidnappers. We cannot keep her here. When Victor finds out, he's going to be livid."

"I did whack her hard on the head," the lady said. "Maybe she will forget what has happened."

"Oh, that's just wonderful," the new voice said. "Who is she? Did she have ID on her?"

"No," Bruce said. "She didn't have a purse on her."

"Has she seen your faces?"

"She may have seen mine earlier," the female said.

Jessica thought for a moment. All she could remember was that she had shoulder length dark red colored hair. She was too scared to notice anything more.

"Where is she?"

"In the utility closet," Bruce said.

"You put her in a closet?" the man was getting upset again. His anger frightened her.

"Where else could we put her? Keep her in the van at Jack's house?" Bruce asked.

"No," the man said. "Okay." The man's voice was slightly calmer. She could hear movement. He must be pacing. "Blindfold her and bring her to my office."

Jessica quickly scooted back to her corner in the room. The door unlocked and then the woman came in still wearing the ski mask. She did indeed have red hair as it wasn't tucked nicely inside her mask. In one hand she held the blindfold and in the other she had the gun.

"Let's put this back on you," she said. "We need to talk to you."

Jessica didn't struggle this time as the woman put the blindfold back over her eyes and stood her up. She was guided carefully out of the room and down a hallway then the floor turned from tile to carpet.

"Step down," she instructed. "There are three steps."

Jessica carefully stepped down as the woman helped her. The television sounded much closer now and it was indeed a football game playing. *The man named Bruce must be watching T.V.* She thought to herself. They continued walking a few more steps and then entered another room, but not before Jessica bumped into the doorframe. It was warmer in this room. A soothing musky scent of a man's cologne filled the room. The smell was comforting. The woman maneuvered Jessica in the room. She bumped against something hard and the woman put her hands on Jessica's shoulders and pushed her down into a chair. It felt like an office chair, like the ones her dad had in his office.

"Don't scream," the new man said calmly. His warm hand caressed her cheek. Jessica jumped and started to sob. "I'm not going to hurt you," he said softly. "I'm going to take the tape off your mouth, okay?"

Jessica nodded and tried not to cry, but her shivers were still there.

His warm hand gently found the corner of the tape and slowly pulled the tape up from around her mouth. Jessica quickly licked her lips. She could feel dryness in her throat and if she wasn't careful, she could possibly vomit. She continued shaking.

"Connie, get her a drink," the man ordered to the woman.

The blindfold remained on her eyes. Not seeing what was around her frightened her. Yet his soothing voice seemed to calm her. She felt something warm and heavy move over her shoulders. It was a man's suit coat. The smell of a man's cologne lingered on the garment. Even though the jacket provided warmth, it was the unknown that was frightening her. Was this man going to kill her like Bruce told the woman earlier?

THREE

Sean gazed upon this poor, scared girl. Her wavy brown hair was messed up from the struggle. She looked to be about early twenties; hopefully not younger. Why in the world would she have been in the alley? He could see her shivering from fear and the only thing he could think of was to put his jacket over her shoulders. Once he did, her shivering subsided a bit. He leaned up against his desk and stared at this girl.

"My friends here did something really stupid," Sean spoke softly to not scare her. "They grabbed you when they should not have."

"I want to go home," the girl whispered. "I won't tell."

"What is your name?" Sean continued to speak softly to her.

"J-J-Jessica."

"Jessica," Sean said as he took the water from Connie when she returned to the office. "I have some water here, take a sip." He placed the glass next to her lips and she opened her mouth to allow the cool water to flow inside. She took a few good drinks and a little bit spilled down her chin. He reached over and wiped it away with his hand.

"Do you live in Winslow?" Sean asked her, wiping his hand on his pants.

"Yes," Jessica answered. "Are we not in Winslow?"

"You don't need to know where we are." Sean provided her with another sip of water.

"How long have I been here?" Jessica panicked. "What time is it?"

"Well, it is about 10:30 p.m.," Sean told her. "I'm sure someone may have reported you missing by now, right? Do you live with your parents or roommate?"

"No, I live by myself." A tear rolled down from under the blindfold. "I usually go to dinner at my parents' house on Saturday. I'm sure they know I'm missing."

"Why were you in the alley?"

"My car broke down. I was on the back street behind the strip mall. I was going to call my dad to come get me, but I didn't want to bother him in his meeting. My mom usually has meetings on Saturday afternoon, too, so I didn't know if I'd be able to get a hold of her. I accidentally locked my keys and purse in the car because I was so mad at my car for breaking down. My cell phone was in there," the poor girl rambled on.

"What does your mom do that would make her not want to help her daughter?"

"S-she's involved with city council stuff," Jessica answered with a cute stutter.

Sean put the glass on his desk. He studied her a little more closely and he leaned a bit forward towards her.

"What is your last name, Jessica?"

She hesitated in answering. He wondered if she was going to lie to him. But why would she lie? If her parents had reported her missing, she'd be all over the morning news so there would be no need to lie.

"Cook," Jessica whispered.

Sean stood up with haste, moving away from the desk.

"Is your father Mayor Cook?"

Jessica gulped and whispered out a "Yes."

Sean paced his room and glared at Connie and shook his head. He hurried past Jessica, grabbing Connie's arm as they exited his office and practically dragged her over to where Bruce was sitting.

"You kidnapped the Mayor's daughter?" Sean yelled at them.

"We didn't know she was the Mayor's daughter," Connie said as she backed away and sat on the couch next to Bruce.

"This is not good," Sean said. "Police are going to be all over this. Victor is going to be pissed to no end."

"We can drop her off outside of town," Bruce said.

"No." Sean stopped and began thinking. He pointed a finger at Bruce. "Ransom?"

"I thought we didn't want to be kidnappers?" Bruce asked.

"I don't, but her family has money. We can add to the fund. Maybe this might be a way to keep Victor from being upset. I need to think about this," Sean said. "You two go to bed. We have a lot to discuss tomorrow."

"What about her," Connie began. "Take her back to the utility room?"

"Heavens, no," Sean quickly said. "That's no place for the mayor's daughter. Take her to the guest room, next to mine."

Sean followed Connie back into the office. Connie roughly pulled the girl up from the chair. His suit coat fell off her shoulders and into the chair. With her arm on Jessica's she led her to the door. Connie stopped and faced him.

"I'm sorry I messed up."

"Yeah, me too." Sean moved past her and headed to his chair behind the desk. He had a feeling that Connie was planning a 'snuggle time' with him later but this 'mess up' was now a main priority on his mind. He needed to get rid of Jessica, and quickly.

Connie moved Jessica out the door.

"Eight steps. Going up." He heard Connie say to the girl.

"C-can you untie my hands, please?" Jessica voice was shaky. "I don't want to fall."

Sean moved back to the doorway.

"Do it," Sean instructed. "Untie her hands."

Connie ripped apart the tape that was holding Jessica's hands. Once freed, Jessica brought them to the front of her and rubbed them. Her hand reached out to grasp for the handrail and then she began stepping up the stairs slowly.

****

As Jessica climbed the stairs the thought of escaping through the window might be something she could do. She is tiny enough to climb out a window. She would just have to be really quiet and hope that there was a tree she could hold onto to get out. She had to try to escape. The man named Sean didn't seem too awful, but she knew he was just acting nice so she wouldn't cry. The other guy they talked about, Victor, he was the one that scared her now. He must be the leader of this group. She had to find a way to get home.

The woman sat Jessica on a bed and took off the blindfold. Jessica blinked her eyes then wiped them with her hands to remove the tears that still lingered. She was sitting on a very soft Queen-sized bed. A long dresser with a mirror was against the wall. To her left was a window. Hope filled her chest. She would have a chance.

The woman who Sean referred to as Connie opened a drawer and pulled out a silky nightgown and tossed it to her.

"Go to bed," she said. "Don't think of trying to get out, the door will be locked."

She stepped out and closed the door behind her. Jessica stood up and rushed to the window and frantically pulled back the curtains. Shutters were closed over the window from the outside. She began to move her hands around the window to try and open it. The window wouldn't budge. In defeat, she fell back onto the bed and started to cry again. Crying made her head hurt more but she couldn't stop crying. There would be no escaping tonight.

There wasn't a phone in the room, but there was an alarm clock. Jessica turned off the light and curled up on the bed facing the alarm clock. This was going to be a very long night. Maybe security cameras caught her being abducted and maybe police were out looking for her already.

All these possibilities entered her mind making it hard to rest. She laid there looking at the clock as the time moved from 10:45 p.m. to 1:15 a.m. The house went quiet. Her eyes were tired, and they hurt from crying so much. Jessica didn't want to fall asleep for fear of what they might do to her if she did sleep. Would they kill her? Would they violate her body?

Every time she closed her eyes her head pounded more as frightening thoughts entered her mind. The pain in her head was making her stomach feel sick, like a migraine headache that she had a few years ago. She put the blanket that was on the bed around her but refused to change into the nightgown. A light tap on her door startled her.

"Jessica," Sean's soft voice called out to her. "Are you still awake?"

Should I pretend to be asleep? Is he here to kill me? Jessica's thoughts went wild. She hesitated before answering.

"Yes."

"Are you comfortable in there?" He asked.

"My head hurts really badly and I'm hungry," she answered as tears rolled down her face.

"I have some ibuprofen," he said. "Do you want it?"

"Y-yes, please."

There was silence for a few moments and then the door unlocked and opened. The dim light from the room across from hers glowed inside her room. A figure of a man stepped inside the room. The floor creaked as he walked over to the side of the bed. He handed her a glass of water and the pills. She couldn't see his face because of the darkness.

"You aren't drugging me, are you?" Jessica asked nervously before taking the pills.

"No, this is ibuprofen, I promise," he said. "I'll be back with something for you to eat, I'm sure you are hungry."

"I didn't do anything wrong," Jessica said as she popped the pills in her mouth and swallowed them down with the water. "I won't tell anyone. Just let me go."

"I'll let you go," he said. "But not yet." He removed himself from the room, closed the door and re-locked it.

Jessica sat back on the bed and put her knees up by her chest. This day had turned into a complete nightmare. She knew her parents would be looking for her. She just hoped they would be able to find her.

She rubbed the temples of her head and pinched the bridge of her nose to get the headache to go away. She touched the tender spot on the back of her head where that woman hit her. It did feel swollen. If she could just fall asleep, maybe the pain would go away in her head.

The door unlocked again and opened. The man, Sean, walked inside carrying a plate and another glass of water.

"Sorry, it's not much, just a turkey sandwich. I hope you like turkey," he said as he handed her the plate.

"Thank you." She took it from him and nibbled a piece off. It did taste good.

"So, how old are you?" Sean asked making conversation.

"I'm twenty-five," she said in-between bites. "I have a job…well, after this I probably won't since I can't call in sick, it will be a no-show and they will fire me."

He folded his arms across his chest and leaned against the dresser. He let out a small laugh.

"I'm sure they will make an exception in regards to you being kidnapped."

"Do you know where my glasses are?" Jessica asked.

"You wear glasses?" he questioned. "No, I wasn't there when you were taken. They are probably gone."

She took another bite of the sandwich and tried to look at this man. The darkness in the room hid his facial features.

"Are you the same robbers who have been doing all those burglaries in this area?"

"The one and only." His voice boomed with confidence of their accomplishments.

"But you don't take prisoners. At least that is what they said. Why now?"

"Connie messed up," he explained. "Now I'm left to figure out the best way to fix the problem. You cannot be here. You aren't safe here."

"Then let me go!" Jessica pleaded. "I promise, I won't tell anything to the police. I don't even know what you guys look like."

"It's not that easy. You see, there is another guy, named Victor. He knows you are here. He will be here tomorrow night. I need to convince him that you are not a threat and how we can profit from Connie's mistake. Victor is not very nice. I'm warning you now, don't talk back to him."

"Why are you telling me this?" Jessica asked as she took another bite of the sandwich.

"Well, up until now, we have had no one get in our way. You are now going to make it harder for us to stay out of the spotlight. I don't want to see you, or anyone get hurt, so I will do my best to protect you." He backed away from her and towards the door. "Go to sleep, Jessica. If you need something, I'm in the next room, just knock on the wall."

"I-I suppose I s-should thank you for being nice," she stuttered a bit before he got to the door. "I heard that other guy say you would kill that other lady and me, possibly."

He laughed. He had a nice laugh.

"Maybe I get upset every so often when things don't go my way. But I'm not going to hurt you, I can promise you that. I will do all I can to get you out of here safely."

He closed the door behind him as he stepped out. She heard the door lock. She took a deep breath then quickly finished her sandwich and drink. This Victor person sounded scary and she did not want to meet him.

She put the plate on the night stand and pulled the covers back over her. She closed her eyes. *I don't think Trent will be coming for me tonight,* she thought as she began drifting off to sleep.

FOUR

Jessica awoke hearing voices from the other side of the wall. She could tell that it was the television playing the local morning news. The alarm clock said it was just about 8:00 a.m. A little bit of light was shining through the cracks of the outside shutter letting her know it was indeed morning. She survived the night, but would she survive the day? It was Sunday morning and how she wished she was in church with her parents and not here.

She listened closely as a news reporter on the television began making the announcement that Mayor Cook's daughter, Jessica, was missing and that if anyone had any information to contact Winslow Police Department. They also mentioned that her car was found off to the side of the road with her purse and phone inside. Right after that they spoke of a break-in at the jewelry store. They did not believe the two were related.

Jessica's head still hurt, but not as bad as it did the night before. Sleep and ibuprofen did help, thankfully. She wanted to keep sleeping, hoping that this was all just a bad dream. She jumped at the thumping on the door and then the door being unlocked. Jessica quickly sat up causing a throb in her head. That woman was back again. She still had the mask over her face but wore different clothes.

"Come on," she said roughly. "Bathroom break."

Jessica got out of bed and walked to the door slowly. Her mind was still hazy from the bump on her head leaving her a little dizzy.

"Do you have my glasses?" Jessica asked Connie as she stopped at the door.

"No, they fell off of you in the struggle," she said.

"I cannot see very well."

"Well, that is lucky for us," she laughed a little. "Then you cannot identify us."

Connie led her, without the blindfold, to the bathroom across from the room Jessica spent the night in.

"Do you live here?" Jessica asked her since she really didn't see much girl stuff in the bathroom.

"On certain nights," she responded.

Connie closed the door so Jessica could do the wake-up routine. Jessica quickly looked around the room to see if there was anything she could use as a weapon to get out of the house. Nothing but a toilet plunger was available for protection. That would only work if she had a good enough swing, but, she didn't. Her stomach growled. She was hungry and she really hoped they would feed her.

After Jessica washed her hands and face, she pinched her cheeks to try to put color in her face. She tried running her fingers through her long, thick hair, but it was hopeless. She still looked tired, pale and scared. She opened the door and the woman was standing at the other doorway talking to Sean in the other room. Jessica could tell by the way this woman was standing, with her arm stretched up the door frame with her fingers running through the top of her hair that she was in some type of flirt mode. She had seen those movements by Demi at the bank as she observed Demi talking with Trent. From what she could see, the woman's hair was indeed shoulder length and dark red and she had an attractive shape. This gal and Sean must be an item, something like Bonnie and Clyde probably.

Connie pulled the mask quickly back over her face, turned to face her and pointed to the bedroom where she had spent the night.

"Go," the woman said roughly.

Jessica took a few steps until she was in the middle of the hallway and stopped.

"I-I'm on television now, aren't I?" she asked aloud.

"Yes." Sean's deep voice came from the other room. He stepped out into the hallway. He had no mask on. He wore a light blue dress shirt, but it wasn't buttoned yet and it revealed his muscular tanned chest. A dark blue tie hung around his neck. His black slacks fit nicely along his legs. Was he going to church? She didn't recall people at church looking this nice. He seemed too dressed up for a Sunday.

"Sean," Connie whispered to him possibly warning him that his face wasn't covered. He waved her off. His walk showed his confidence. He stood at least a good head taller than she was. She squinted her eyes a bit as he got closer. His chest was the first thing that came into clear view, since it was right in line with her eyes. His chest was well defined, so he must work out on a regular basis. Her eyes glanced up to his face. He had a very short beard. His hair was brown and neatly combed. He smelled fresh from a shower. His lips were slightly puffy, perfect in every way. Her heart beat faster as neared closer to her. How in the world could she be so lucky to be kidnapped by a hunk of a man?

"I've got to go into work today," he said. "Connie here will keep an eye on you. She will feed you and keep you entertained, the best she can. I hope to have some type of plan for your return when I come back. Victor will be stopping by tonight. I need to have something to tell him when he comes."

"I-I'm hungry," Jessica stammered. She really did not know what to say.

"Connie, go get her something to eat," he ordered. Connie snorted a bit as she walked past Jessica.

"I don't like her," Jessica whispered as she watched Connie go down the stairs.

"She is kind of snooty," he said softly. "I'll have a talk with her. She's used to being the only girl here. Now she feels threatened with you being here."

"But she is the one who brought me here. She could have left me."

"I guess it is that soft heart she sometimes has." He walked past Jessica and into the bathroom and grabbed his electric razor. He turned it on and started moving it over his neck and around his short beard.

"Is there a brush or something I can use for my hair?" Jessica asked raking her fingers nervously through her knotted hair. She now suddenly felt very self-conscious to the un-kempt way she looked. She knew she could look better.

"Connie has some girl stuff. You can change clothes and shower," he said. His eyes wandered down her body sending a shiver over her. "Your pants look a bit dirty from the struggle yesterday."

Jessica found her eyes gazing at his open shirt and chest. It was just not right for someone to look this wonderful. He looked as though he was ready for a photo shoot for GQ Magazine. Jessica moved her eyes to his face. She couldn't tell what color his eyes were unless she got really close to him, which she didn't plan to do, but the thought of moving closer caused a flutter in her stomach. From what she could see in her fuzzy state, he was gorgeous. He didn't look old, but he was older than her.

"W-where do you work?" Jessica asked him nervously.

"I work in private security," he replied.

"Aren't you afraid you are telling me too much and I might turn you in?"

"We will see," he said. "Maybe I'm lying to you and I'm really an accountant, or maybe I'm going to a funeral."

He put his razor down and began buttoning his shirt. Jessica couldn't help but just stand there watching him. The scene of him buttoning his shirt made her heart patter with excitement. He looked so much better than Trent ever could. He tied his tie around his neck then splashed some cologne on his cheeks. It was the same smell from the office last night, but a little stronger. He smelled and looked wonderful.

"You look good," Connie said to him as she approached. She handed Jessica a bagel with cream cheese on it. "Don't you think he looks good?" she asked Jessica poking her with her elbow.

Connie must have noticed her staring at him. Jessica could feel her face growing a bit warm.

"I..." Jessica started to stutter again. "I..cannot see very well without my glasses."

"Right." She had a laugh in her voice. "Go eat in your room."

Jessica turned and hurried back to the room but left the door open.

****

Sean grinned as he did notice that this girl, Jessica, was checking him over, even though she'd probably not admit it. Connie moved in closer to him as she straightened his tie a bit more.

"Be nice to her," Sean told Connie.

"Sean, I am."

"Have her shower and give her a change of clothes. You both look about the same size," he said. "She said she needs to brush her hair, too."

"Oh, alright," she sighed out.

"Also, don't keep her locked up in her room all day," he said. "You can uncover your face." He pulled the mask off of Connie's face and gave her a quick kiss.

"But she can identify us, you for sure."

"I don't think she will," Sean whispered to her. "If we treat her well, I bet things will change in our favor. Besides, if things don't work out, we can just bail this joint and go north."

Connie leaned in for another kiss. Sean put his arms around Connie for a quick embrace instead. He was already running a bit behind so no lingering in this position. Besides, it wasn't in his plans to be this close to Connie anyway. She was just a member of this team, not a romantic interest. He stepped away from Connie and stopped in front of the guest bedroom. Jessica sat nibbling on her bagel with her eyes downward to the floor.

"Try and have a good day, Jessica," Sean spoke with encouragement.

"Thank you," Jessica replied lifting her gaze to him.

As Sean left the house, he really hoped that Connie would be nice to her. He hated to keep Jessica as a prisoner and he really wanted her to return to her family so he could continue with his plans. Today was going to be a long day.

He had already received a message this morning that one of his clients was in need of assistance. He would have to put his regular things on hold while he took care of this client. It was going to be hard not to think about Jessica and this problem Connie got them all into. Somehow, he needed to stay focused, that diamond needed to be found and quickly. Jessica needed to leave.

****

Jessica sat staring at the window in the bedroom. Her mind tried to come up with a way to break through the shutter without being heard. How far would the drop be? Would she break a leg in the fall? Her thoughts were interrupted as she heard movement outside her room. Connie stepped inside and motioned with her hand to come her way.

"Come on," she said. "Go take a shower. I left a few of my outfits in there for you to wear so we can wash your clothes."

Jessica slowly stood then followed her out of the room. Everything seemed so weird, because in the movies the prisoners were locked away in some dark cold room all the time while being starved and beat, during captivity. Never did it show they were given shower breaks. It confused her as to why they were being nice to her.

"Is that other guy, Victor, mean?" Jessica asked nervously, trying to make small talk.

"His temper is worse than Sean's," she said. "Victor doesn't live here. This is the club house, I suppose you could say. Sean mostly lives here. Sean is in control of this place until Victor shows up, then Victor is in charge."

"Is he going to hurt me?" Jessica asked.

"Sean or Victor?"

"Victor." Jessica couldn't help but wonder if Sean would hurt her too, but, Victor was who she was mostly nervous about right now.

"No clue. Maybe he'll be in a good mood tonight. After all, we did come back with a good load of jewelry for him."

"Why do you do this?"

"Duh, for money." Connie laughed.

"Don't you have a real job? It seems that Sean has a job, or he's going to church?" Jessica observed aloud.

"Church?" Connie burst out laughing. "The walls would crumble if he walked inside a church, with all the bad things he's done. The guys all have legitimate jobs. It keeps them looking normal. Go shower. I've told you too much."

Connie pulled the door closed and left Jessica alone inside the bathroom.

The warm water streamed over her body allowing her to relax. It was very refreshing. She had a chance to feel around her head at that whack she received from Connie. The bump was tender and as far as she could tell it wasn't getting any bigger so it would heal. At least she wasn't seeing stars or feeling sick to her stomach anymore.

After drying off, Jessica reached for the clothes that Connie left for her to put on. There was a skimpy pair of underwear and matching black bra. She felt creepy putting another person's under clothes on. Surprisingly, though, they fit. The Levi's that she was given were tight fitting and had slash cuts in the legs. The tee shirt was purple long sleeved with a low rounded neck that hugged to her chest tightly. Jessica opened the door and stepped out. Connie was sitting on the stairs flipping through a magazine waiting for her. The ski mask was off, and her shoulder-length red hair curved around her face.

"Not bad," Connie said looking up from the magazine. "They fit."

"Amazingly," Jessica commented. "A little tight, though."

"No, that is how you are to wear them," Connie said. "So, do you keep your hair curly all the time?"

"I've really never known any other way to do my hair," Jessica answered. "Growing up, my mom always liked my curly hair so she really wouldn't do much to it."

"Do you?"

"Not all the time." Jessica ran her fingers through her hair. "It's naturally wavy, though. I don't really have a choice."

"Sure, you do. Come here," she said as she pulled her back into the bedroom. She dug through the dresser and pulled out a few items like a blow dryer and a flat curling iron. She pulled the chair over and said, "Sit."

"You are going to do my hair?"

"I'm being nice to you," Connie said branding a fake smile. "Sean told me to be nice to you. Besides, I'm not much of a babysitter. So, you have a job somewhere? Do you have a boyfriend?"

Jessica sat down on the chair and thought of Trent.

"Yes and no," Jessica finally admitted sadly. "There is a guy I have been watching for over seven years now. He doesn't even know I exist. But I know he does."

"Why? Is he out of your league?"

"I went to school with him and now both he and I work at the same bank. He's just really cute. He was on the basketball team when we were in high school. Now he just looks great but doesn't even know I exist," Jessica explained.

"Have you talked to him?"

"Oh, no!" Jessica said quickly. "I don't talk to guys very well. I get all nervous and I stutter."

"You were talking okay with Sean this morning. It's not that bad."

Connie turned on the hair blower and started drying Jessica's hair. She pulled a brush through Jessica's hair. She felt like she was in a beauty salon.

"How long have you known him?" Jessica yelled over the blower.

"Victor or Sean?"

"Sean."

"Almost a year ago he joined the team. I'm not sure where Bruce found him. But Sean had some good skills that Victor wanted. Bruce is my brother. He was the other guy last night that put the duct tape on your legs. Jack was the driver, you haven't seen him yet. We've been working with Victor for three years."

"You don't look that old," Jessica said. "You look maybe a little older than I am."

"How old are you?" Connie asked as she continued pulling the brush through Jessica's hair.

"I'm twenty-five."

"I'm twenty-seven. When I first helped on a heist, the thrill was better than a first kiss. I just had to be involved."

"I wouldn't know," Jessica mumbled under her breath.

"You've never been kissed?" Connie almost laughed. "Girlfriend, we need to get you a date with this guy."

"So, do you think if I do something else with my hair that maybe Trent will notice me?"

"Does this Trent have a girlfriend?"

Jessica thought of Demi. She had no idea if they were seeing each other.

"He might. He flirts with a girl at work all the time. I'm sure they've gone out."

Connie plugged in the flat iron and brushed Jessica's long hair straight, pulling out all the tangles.

"Well, you might get his attention if you changed up your looks. The outfit you were wearing when we grabbed you, is that how you dress all the time?"

Jessica thought of the tan pants and the flowery top she had on earlier. She nodded her head.

"I have to dress nice when I work at the bank."

"Well, I think the pants were a bit larger on you and the top was not flattering at all. So, yes, if you changed what you wore you might draw more attention to yourself." Connie picked up the flat iron. "I've got an idea. I'm going to make you up so you can see what you could look like to attract Trent."

"You don't need to do that. Remember, I'm the prisoner here."

"No, I feel like I am," Connie breathed deeply out in sadness. "I can't leave because you are here. My fault, I know. So, I might as well have fun while I'm here."

Connie pulled the iron through Jessica's hair. Jessica was not sure how well this activity was going to turn out, but it did seem a little fun. Maybe today wouldn't be so bad after all.

FIVE

Jessica stood in front of a full-length mirror in the bedroom admiring her new look. Was this really her? Connie had managed to straighten and style her long dark hair and also put makeup on her. Connie stood back with a grin on her face as she admired her work of art. Jessica was surprised to see that she didn't look like what she did yesterday morning going to work. She looked pretty and dare she say, sexy.

"I don't believe it," Jessica gasped. "I look awesome."

"You look Hot!" Connie said with a smile. "I really should be a beautician, oh, and, one final touch." Connie took out a perfume bottle and sprayed it around Jessica. The scent was pleasant but not overbearing.

"So, now how do I talk to him?" Jessica's voice filled with enthusiasm.

"Well, looking like this, the guy will most likely come talk to you," she laughed. "I think you need to feel more confident in yourself. You are not ugly. I think you've been hiding behind outdated clothes and hairstyles."

"I'm the mayor's daughter. I cannot look like a wild woman. I cannot embarrass my dad."

"Isn't this his last year in office?" Connie asked.

"Yes, but-"

"No buts. You are twenty-five years old and time to make a change. You've got the body, find the clothes and flaunt it." Connie interrupted her.

"If I make it out of here alive, I guess I better go shopping then," Jessica said.

"You'll make it out of here alive, I'm sure of it."

Connie began cleaning up the make-up.

"My friend at work keeps telling me to go talk to Trent, but I can't. I become accident prone and act stupid when I'm around him, or any guy for that matter."

"You need to practice." Connie nodded. "Talk to Sean. He's gorgeous. He can help you overcome your fears so you can approach Trent."

"Oh, that wouldn't be a good idea," she disagreed. "He's your guy."

"Sean and I aren't really together. It would be nice, but he seems to have other things on his mind all the time and he makes excuses a lot to not be intimate with me. Maybe I'm not his type. But still, he lets me kiss him, so that's a plus."

Jessica followed Connie downstairs. They took her clothes into the room where they kept her in yesterday to wash the clothes. The room was indeed by a door that probably led to outside.

Connie gave her a little tour of the house. There was a small bathroom across the hall from the utility room where she was taken last night. The kitchen wasn't that big, but the dining room had a large oak table that seated at least eight people. A few steps down from the kitchen were a large living room area and the front door. A room just off the living room had a closed door. She could only assume that was the office that they brought her to when she talked to Sean. The steps across the living room lead upstairs, where the three bedrooms were. Her eyes went back to the front door. If Connie was distracted, maybe she would make a run for it.

"Are we even in Winslow?" Jessica asked hoping to get a better idea as to where they were.

"No," she replied. "That's all I will tell you."

Jessica went and sat down at the couch and picked up the newspaper that was sitting there, it was the same newspaper that was on her dad's desk Friday night. The paper was opened up to the article about that missing diamond necklace called the Midnight Star. The diamond necklace sparkled in the photo. It was breathtaking. She'd never seen anything like it.

"Did you guys steal this?" Jessica asked as she turned the photo towards Connie.

"I'm not at liberty to tell." She smiled sneakily as if she was hiding the truth.

"You did, I just know it. Was it hard to take it? I heard there was tons of security and it has baffled the police."

"Something like that takes a lot of planning," Connie began moving up to the kitchen.

"What do you do with the jewelry?"

"Victor takes it and we get our cut eventually. Let's not talk about that. I've told you way too much. I'm probably going to get in trouble for saying anything to you." Connie opened the fridge and looked around. "Dang it, Sean!" She slammed the fridge door cussing. "He didn't go shopping and there is no food in the fridge for lunch except grape jelly to make Peanut Butter and Jelly sandwiches. I don't want that for lunch."

"That's okay, if that's all you have." Jessica wasn't picky. She knew what type of food she ate living alone. If Sean lived here alone, he probably didn't have many things to create meals with. She was pretty sure he ate out a lot.

"Nope," Connie said picking up her cell phone and dialed a number.

If Connie was ordering food for delivery then maybe she could slip a note to the driver telling him that she was being kidnapped and to go for help. Yes, that would be a perfect plan. Excitement filled her body.

"Hey, Babe," Connie said on the phone. "Oh, she's fine. I gave her a makeover. She looks great, if I have to say so myself." She paused. "It's all good, Hun. Look, I'm calling because you didn't go shopping yesterday and there is no food in the house. We are getting hungry. Can you come home for lunch and bring us some food?" She paused again. "Oh, sweet, we will see you in a bit then."

Connie hung up her phone and smiled a victorious smile.

"Sean will pick up some pizza for us. He's coming home for lunch." She laughed. "I think he's afraid of what I did to you."

Jessica placed the newspaper back on the coffee table. Discouragement filled her chest. Her escape plan was not going to work. She would have to think of something else. Maybe if she acted like a friend to Connie, she would be able to convince her to let her go before Sean got home.

"So how do I gain confidence?" Jessica asked.

"Be bold in how you talk. Flirt with the guys. It's okay to blush. The guys actually like it when girls blush."

"I cannot be bold, I'm shy."

"Let what comes out of your mouth just happen, don't stop it. You look smart, so say smart things."

"But it's just being in their presence that messes up my speech. My mind goes blank. I trip over my tongue," Jessica admitted.

"Like I said earlier; talk to Sean. Practice on him."

Jessica closed her eyes and rested her head back on the couch. Besides trying to figure out how to get out of here, being without her glasses was for sure the cause of her headache now.

An hour slowly passed by and Jessica's stomach was growling a bit louder. She had sipped on water hoping that it would stop her stomach from making too much noise. She rested her eyes off and on considering she didn't get a lot of sleep last night. Her eyes jarred open when she heard the back door open and the smell of pizza flowing through the room. Her gaze turned to the kitchen where she saw Sean putting down a pizza box.

"Oh, that smells so good," Jessica said as she approached the table.

"Whoa!" Sean's gaze stopped upon her as he surveyed her over from top to bottom. "Jessica?"

"Umm..."Jessica started to feel uncomfortable with his lustful gaze. "Yes."

"Wow." He smiled with a twinkle glowing in his eyes. "You look great...really great."

"The pizza looks better," Jessica quickly said as she reached for a piece of pizza.

"Didn't I do a great job?" Connie cheerfully said. "I think I did."

"She was good before, but man..." Sean shook his head. "Hot. Maybe Victor won't be too upset tonight after he sees her."

Jessica stuffed the pizza in her mouth.

"Slow down." He laughed. "I don't want you to choke. You are a valuable piece, I cannot lose you."

"She's been kind of fun today," Connie told him. "We've had a lot of girl talk."

"Don't corrupt her, Connie." Sean reached for a piece of pizza, too.

"No, I'm not corrupting…I'm teaching her."

"I doubt you need to teach her anything." Sean kept his lustful eyes on her as he took a bite of the pizza.

Jessica tried not to look at him, but she could still feel his eyes watching her.

"I'm going to leave and go back to my place later," Connie told Sean. "How long is Victor going to be here?"

"It depends on what he wants to discuss," Sean replied. Sean's watch beeped. "I've got to head back. I've got tons of stuff happening today. I'll be back at 5:00." He leaned over and kissed Connie on the forehead and he took another look at Jessica and smiled. He grabbed another piece of pizza then turned and walked away.

Jessica let out a long sigh as he closed the door. His gaze made her a little uncomfortable, but she also felt a tingling feeling in her stomach. It felt good to be noticed, even if it was from the one holding her captive.

Later in the afternoon, Connie and Jessica sat on the floor in the front room looking through her stash of fashion magazines. Connie was pointing out the do's and don'ts for what to wear.

"So, do you use your cut of the money to buy clothes?" Jessica asked her.

"Yes. In fact, I did buy me a new car a few months back." Connie smiled.

"Aren't you afraid of getting caught? It is very dangerous what you guys do."

"I like the rush," she said, "the excitement of living on the edge. Sean has helped us a lot in feeling confident in what we are doing and the things to look for to make us stop and turn away from the loot. He's a good teacher." She flipped a page. "So, do you do anything fun?"

"No," Jessica said sadly. "I visit my parents' every other day, but I mostly just go home and read."

"Reading what?"

"Romance novels." Jessica laughed softly. "The guys are safe in there."

"Oh, but it's so much more fun loving a real man." Connie smiled big. "You should put the books down and do something completely wild and against the rules."

"Like what?" Jessica questioned.

"You ought to come with us on a heist. That would get your heart racing."

"Oh, no." Jessica shook her head quickly. "I cannot do that. That is against the law. Besides, with my luck; I'd get us all caught. I don't want to go to jail."

"You won't get us caught. We have a secret weapon…Sean."

"How is he your secret weapon?"

"He knows security systems very well." she grinned.

"Well, I'm not going to break the law."

"Suit yourself," she said. "Okay, let's talk Trent. Once you show up at work wearing your new outfit and hair done to perfection, you are going to need to get his attention."

"Like how?"

"Hmm. How do you walk?" Connie put down her magazine.

"What?"

"Get up and walk for me." Connie motioned her hands for Jessica to stand up.

Jessica stood up. She had the magazine she was looking at still in her hands. She held it to her body and began walking across the room. This was completely stupid. She really never walked around at the bank so why would she want to walk past Trent?

"Lift you head," Connie ordered. "Be confident. You are beautiful and sexy."

Jessica lifted her head a bit higher and smiled as she repeated the words in her head of 'You are beautiful.'

Convincing herself was probably the hardest thing to do to gain confidence.

"Music!" Connie quickly stood up. "Think of a beat while you walk." She went over to the stereo and rummaged through the CD's. She grabbed one out and put it in the player. "Oh, this is perfect music to strut to." She pushed play and it began playing an upbeat song with lots of bass and drums. Connie cranked up the volume.

Jessica was seeing a very normal side of Connie. Even though she was a thief, she also was just a girl who wanted to have some fun. Jessica continued to walk with the song playing loudly over the speakers.

"Shake your hips when you walk." Connie stood up and started to walk with her. She hooked her arm through Jessica's and walked the floor like they were heading to some fancy dance club. Jessica laughed as she swung her hips to the beat as she walked with Connie. "Shake it, baby."

Jessica found herself singing along with the songs while both girls were strutting and dancing to the music. This was indeed the strangest thing she'd ever done. For a bit, she had forgotten that she was kidnapped and instead she felt like she was at a girls' sleepover. It felt good to laugh and be silly. It took the stress away of being held hostage.

Connie taught her a few dance moves that were a bit on the seductive side, dirty dancing is what she called it. Maybe if she got the chance to actually go on a date with Trent, she could use these moves. She longed to dance with Trent while he held her in his strong arms.

She practiced the rolling of her hips and moving her arms over her body as she thought of Trent but then someone grabbed her arm and twirled her around. Sean had Connie in one arm and was pulling Jessica in to him with the other. Her heart beat out of control and her legs turned to jelly. She was too caught up in the moment that she didn't even hear Sean come home. Her feet stopped moving.

Connie kept dancing with Sean, she moved closer to him to do a little dirty dancing with him. Sean's face looked as though he was completely enjoying this moment. She felt Sean's warm arm around her waist.

"Don't stop," Connie told Jessica. "Keep dancing.

Jessica couldn't do it. She felt her cheeks warming up as Sean gazed into her eyes. Her stomach tingled with excitement as he let go of Connie and pulled her closer into him. With her hand still in his, he moved her hands to his shoulders and put his hands on her waist and swayed to the music with her.

"I would have come home earlier if I had known there as a party going on." Sean reached back up to her hands and then gave Jessica a quick twirl.

The music stopped and Sean released her. Jessica let out a fast sigh. Jessica's eyes dropped to the floor and her cheeks were hot from embarrassment.

"Oh, you know," Connie began, "we were just practicing confidence building skills."

"Dancing is a good confidence builder." Sean pulled off his tie. "Do you go out to clubs a lot?"

"No," Jessica said shyly.

"She's stuck on a guy who doesn't know she exists." Connie spilled the beans. How could she look at him now? Jessica was really embarrassed.

"Is he blind?" Sean asked. "Jess, you are extremely hot. How could he not see you?"

Jessica looked up quickly and met his gaze. No one ever called her Jess before. It sounded weird, but she liked it, especially coming from him.

"He has a girlfriend," Connie continued speaking.

"Possibly," Jessica corrected.

"Oh, well, he flirts with another girl at the bank. He just doesn't see her," Connie added.

"Well, when you go home and look like this, he will see you for sure." Sean looked her over again with a smile.

"I'm too smart. I'm shy and I'm just the mayor's dorky daughter." Jessica argued with him.

"Stop that." Sean moved in closer to her. "Being smart and shy is not a bad thing. Being a dorky daughter is, but you aren't dorky. You are a smart and sexy daughter."

Did he just call her sexy? Jessica gulped nervously.

"I have no clue how to make conversation," Jessica said honestly. "I actually have nothing in common with him. I need to just forget him and move on."

"Don't give up yet," Connie pleaded. "I've worked so hard to get you looking like this. Give him the chance to take a good look at you."

"I think it's time to rebel," Sean said with a chuckle. "Go be the woman you want to be."

"But you don't understand." Jessica plopped back down on the couch. "I cannot embarrass my parents because they are in the spotlight all the time."

"So, kidnapping you probably wasn't a good thing then?" Connie laughed. "They are now in the spotlight again."

"They are very worried about you," Sean added being very serious.

"How do you know they are worried?" Jessica leaned forward on the couch.

"I've seen a few different news conferences today. They are begging for information." Sean unbuttoned a few buttons on his shirt.

Jessica's eyes moved to his neck that was now exposed. Her mouth watered a bit. She needed to stop thinking about him this way.

"A-are you going to give them some?" Jessica quickly asked trying to get her mind off of his neck.

"You seemed to be having a good time here. Are you sure you want to go home?" Sean smiled.

The back door opened startling Jessica. She quickly looked back to the kitchen and in walked another man. He was tall with broad shoulders and jet black hair that hung to his neckline. He was carrying a box that smelled of Chinese takeout.

"Dinner time," he said as he came inside. He paused. "Did I interrupt something?"

"Just waiting for an answer," Sean said still looking intently at Jessica.

Jessica stood up. "I don't want dinner to get cold."

"I'm lost," the man said. "Who is she?"

"Jessica," Connie said with a smile. "The girl we grabbed last night."

"Wow, she didn't look like that yesterday," the man said smiling and looking her over. "I think we scored big on this one. Oh, hey, I found something in the van." He reached in and pulled from his pocket a pair of glasses.

"My glasses!" Jessica quickly reached for them and put them on. "Oh, I thought I lost them."

"Jess, that's Bruce," Sean said as he passed by her and went to the cupboard to bring some plates to the table. "Connie's brother."

Jessica nodded to Bruce and sat down at the dining room table. Sean put the plates on the table and pulled out some bottled water from the pantry. Sean sat down next to Jessica. An uneasy feeling arrived in her stomach again. The nearness of Sean, taking in the musky scent of his cologne made her breathing quicker and she began picking at her food.

"Do you like Chinese food?" Sean asked her as he passed the Lo Mein to her.

"Yes, I love Chinese food." Jessica's hands shook as she took the container from Sean.

"You just acted like you weren't hungry there for a minute."

"Just confused," Jessica said honestly. "You guys are just being too nice to me and yet you are keeping me hostage. Confusing, don't you think?"

"Very," Sean admitted as he gave her a wink. "We aren't kidnappers, so we really are quite new to this. If we ever do this again, I'm sure we will be harder on the person we take."

Jessica shook her head. These people were weird, but so normal. While they ate, they spoke of normal things like work, weather, cars, and sports. Every once in a while Jessica would comment something as she felt it was needed. Mostly, she just listened. This group was not going to hurt her. She could feel that now. They were just thieves and she was okay with that. Everything was going to be alright. However, that still didn't stop her mind from thinking of a way to get out of here. The front door would have to be the only way out.

As they were cleaning up, Jessica heard the garage door opening. She looked to the back door in a panic. Her heart began to race. This must be Victor. She almost forgot he was coming by.

Sean approached her. He brought his hands to her glasses and removed them carefully. He reached for the blindfold that was sitting on the counter and placed it over her eyes.

"Sorry," Sean whispered to her. "No peeking."

"Is he going to hurt me?" Jessica started to shake.

"I won't let him," Sean whispered again as he placed his warm hands on her shoulders. "Connie, come get her and take her to the couch."

A soft hand took hold of Jessica's arm. She could smell the perfume of Connie. Jessica was led to the couch. Her stomach twisted in fear and her hands began to sweat. She quickly folded her arms around her for comfort. The sound of the back door opening sent a chill down her spine. Jessica said a silent prayer that everything was going to be alright.

SIX

Sean could sense the change in Jessica's mood as she heard the garage door opening. Her face went pale. He had notified Victor the night before about the new addition to the group. As expected, Victor was not pleased at all. Jessica was a distraction to him, and he needed to get rid of her quickly. Finding the missing diamond was top priority. He knew Victor had it, but where?

Victor stepped into the kitchen, closing the back door, and paused looking around. Sean greeted him by the door.

"She's blindfolded," Sean reassured. "You're safe."

"Connie!" Victor called out.

Connie scurried to the kitchen. She was nervous, Sean could tell.

"Yes," she said in a shaky voice.

"Why...just tell me why you had to pick up baggage?" Victor asked.

"She caught us," Connie said. "We came out and she was there. I panicked. I didn't know what to do."

"But now she's here so what are you going to do about it?" Victor asked glaring at Connie.

"I-I," Connie began to stammer in her words.

"Ransom," Sean spoke up. "She's the mayor's daughter. I think we can get a little something for her."

Victor's gaze moved to Sean. Sean didn't feel uneasy at all. Even though Victor was the same height and size as him, Victor didn't intimidate him. Victor's arrogance showed the others he was in charge, but Sean had his own secrets and knew he could out-win Victor any day.

When Sean found his way into this gang through Bruce, he knew Victor would accept him, considering their team was down a guy. The skill set that he had, knowing how to bypass security systems, was very valuable to Victor. He wasn't there when Victor took the diamond, but he would be there to get it back.

"Ransom?" Victor scratched his pointy chin. "We aren't kidnappers. Why start now? Can't we just drop her off in the desert somewhere? Kill her out there and leave her body?"

Sean heard Jessica suck in a deep breath and hold back a sob.

"We aren't killers, either," Sean said. "She has no clue where she is so there would be no way for her to lead the police back here."

"She has seen your faces. You all have not been very smart."

"We will be long gone by the time she talks to the police," Sean reassured.

Victor walked past Sean and down the stairs to where Jessica sat. He followed Victor down into the living room. Jessica had her arms tightly folded around her. Bruce sat across from her in the recliner. He held a gun in his hands. Victor reached out and touched Jessica's side of the face, she jumped. Sean so badly wanted to push Victor away and tell him to leave her alone, but he didn't want to add suspicion to anyone.

"Or, I just keep her for myself," Victor said grinning. "She looks pretty sweet if you ask me."

Jessica whimpered.

"She's a little feisty," Sean lied. "Has a mouth on her at times." *Yes, she had a mouth on her, a mouth with perfect puffy kissing lips.* Wait, where did that thought come from? He shook his head to get that thought out of his mind.

"Oh, I can tame that," Victor moved his thumb across her lips. Jessica turned her face away quickly in disgust.

"She's worth a lot more in money," Sean quickly said. "Let us work up the deal. $30,000 or $40,000?" He knew that money was a good way to deal with Victor.

"Ah, but she would be so lovely wrapped in my arms." Victor smiled as his eyes wandered over her body, "as well as adorned in jewelry."

"Come," Sean said, "Let's go to the office and have a drink and discuss business." Sean began walking to the office. Victor hesitated in front of Jessica and then he turned and followed Sean into the office. Before closing the door to the office Sean glanced at Jessica who was shivering from fear. Poor girl shouldn't be involved in this.

Victor and Sean sat down at the desk. Sean reached under the desk and pulled out the duffle bag that Bruce and Connie acquired from their heist yesterday. He handed it to Victor. Victor unzipped the bag and looked carefully through the stash pulling diamond necklaces and other pieces of jewelry out to examine closer.

"Not bad. Looks like they cleaned that little shop out." Victor laughed.

"There's at least $20,000 worth of jewels there," Sean said. "When do they get the cash?"

"I'll take these and examine them and get them ready to sell. Maybe in a week they will be compensated."

"Any buyers on the Midnight Star?" Sean asked calmly.

Victor gave him a glance of curiosity.

"You still think I have it, huh?" Victor eyes turned dark and serious. "You know, you won't get a cut of it."

"Just curious if you found a buyer."

"It's still too hot," Victor said. "*If* I have it, it's not going anywhere yet."

That was enough proof for Sean to know that Victor did have it. Now he needed to find out where it was and to get his hands on it. Victor needed to be caught and he was willing to be the one to set him up to be caught.

"So, you don't think Miss Mayor's Daughter is worth my time?" Victor asked, standing up from the chair. He wandered over to the mini bar and poured himself a shot of whiskey.

"She's too young and innocent," Sean said. "She would fight you all the way and resent you forever."

"But it would be fun." Victor drank the whiskey down quickly. "For at least an hour."

"No," Sean said shaking his head. "Let's turn her in for money. If we keep her around, she will ruin our plans, slow us down. She will get us caught."

"True." Victor put the glass down on the table. "Find out a way to pass her off without getting caught but also getting the money." Victor stood up. "I'm leaving her to you to take care of quickly."

"She'll be gone soon," Sean said standing up and pushing the bag towards Victor. Victor reached in his jacket pocket and pulled out a money envelope and handed it to Sean.

"Divide it up how you feel," Victor said. "I'll leave you to babysitting."

Victor swung open the door and glared at Connie.

"Don't do this again, Constance," Victor warned. "Get rid of the mess, all of you."

Sean walked with Victor to the back door.

"Wednesday night," Victor said pulling out a card from his pocket. "Eleven o'clock."

Sean took the card and nodded. Victor was giving him instructions for the next hit. He was getting tired of doing these heists for Victor. Victor was fully capable of doing them himself. He figured it was a way to keep earning his trust with Victor.

Somehow he needed to now find a way to get rid of Jessica before Wednesday. Victor turned and left through the back door. The tension was thick, everyone stayed silent until they heard Victor drive away and the garage door close.

Connie was the first to exhale.

"Oh, man, I really thought I was a goner," she said.

Sean walked down to Jessica and removed her blindfold. Her mascara had smeared a bit from the tears she was holding back. Sean touched her cheek lightly then he moved his hand under her eye to wipe the smeared mascara off her face.

"You don't need to worry about him," Sean said. "I think I've moved his attention away from you. His main interest is money."

Jessica nodded, not saying anything.

"Well, my babysitting is done. I'm going to go home." Connie picked up her purse. "I'll be back tomorrow morning so you can go to work."

Connie slipped her arms around Sean and gave him a kiss. When she pulled away, he could see Jessica's head quickly move to look away. Connie meant nothing to him. He was just using her; he admitted that to himself a while ago. He needed to keep Connie trusting him, to get answers about Victor.

"Be good, girlfriend," Connie said to Jessica and then strutted out the back door.

Bruce put his gun away and turned on the football game and reclined on the chair. Jessica was looking uneasy and still breathing quickly. He figured it was due to the fact she was now alone with two men.

Jessica stood up and went into the kitchen to get a drink and then she grabbed her glasses and put them on. She twisted her hair to one side which he figured was a nervous habit she had. Connie did an amazing job on dolling Jessica up. The outfit Jessica wore accented her curves rather nicely. He felt guilty thinking sexy thoughts about her, but hey, he was only human.

He watched her as she went to the sink and began washing the glasses and forks that were used at dinner time.

"What are you doing?" He asked joining her in the kitchen.

"Washing dishes."

"Not your job to do," he said pulling her away from the sink.

"Look, I'm bored. Don't get me wrong, I'm very thankful that you are being nice to me, feeding me and stuff, but I need something to do to pass the time."

"You are a guest —"

"That cannot leave," Jessica finished for him. "I think that makes me more of a prisoner."

Bruce let out a hoot from the touchdown that was made on the television. Jessica looked down towards him.

"Does he live here?" she whispered to him.

"He thinks he does." Sean laughed. "Both Connie and Bruce have rooms here, but they also have their own places. Do you want me to send him home?"

"No," Jessica said with nervousness in her voice. "I don't know."

"Let him hang out till the game is finished then I'll tell him to leave," Sean suggested.

Jessica took the wash cloth and began wiping off the table. He couldn't help but admire her body as it stretched across the table to wipe it down. It provided him a nice view of her backside. He shook his head again to try to remove those thoughts. Why did she have to be so beautiful?

"Come to my office when you are done," Sean told her. Walking away from her was probably the best thing to do right now to clear his thoughts of wanting to hold her again in his arms, close like they were dancing.

Once in his office, he put the money that was left on the table in a safe under his desk. He didn't have plans on giving the money to Bruce and Connie right away. The longer he held onto it, the more upset the two would get with Victor, and that was what he wanted them to do. Just as he closed the safe Jessica walked in. She looked around at all the books that were lined in the bookcase on the side of the wall. He let her gaze over everything then he asked,

"Do you like to read?"

"Yes," she walked over to the bookshelf and touched the books gingerly. The books he had on this bookshelf were about jewelry, security systems, as well as a few actual novels of crime and mystery. "But a lot of these titles don't interest me," Jessica added turning back to Sean.

"What do you like to read?"

"Romance novels," Jessica said looking down to the floor. "You know, girl stuff."

He chuckled. "So, you like the hot steamy books, huh? I would never have guessed you for liking that." He motioned to the chair. "Have a seat."

Jessica sat across the desk from him. Her hair looked silky and soft. It hung over to the right side of her shoulder. He could smell Connie's perfume that was sprayed on her earlier. It smelled better on Jessica than it did on Connie.

"It's not about the steamy scenes," Jessica said, "It's the love the two share."

"A romantic." Sean smiled. "I like that."

Sean picked up his pen and from the notebook he found a blank sheet of paper.

"So, what shall we say in your ransom note?" He asked.

"I cannot write my own ransom," Jessica gasped in surprise.

"How much do you think you are worth?" He looked deep into her stunning blue eyes. He could get lost in those eyes if he allowed himself. He knew there was no price for her beauty.

"What?" She laughed nervously. "I don't know."

"Let's see," He put the pen against the paper, and he began speaking as he wrote. "We have your daughter." He looked at Jessica and winked. "I'm pretty sure you want her back. We do not plan on hurting your daughter, but we will if you don't follow these rules. 1) We are requesting..." He paused and thought for a moment. "$50,000 in unmarked cash in exchange for your daughter."

Jessica sucked in a surprised breath. Her eyes went large.

"2) Mrs. Cook will be the one who will drop off the money. 3) Drop off will be Wednesday afternoon at 2:15 p.m. at a location only told to Mrs. Cook on Wednesday around 1:50 p.m. 4) Lastly, no police or detectives. If these rules are not met, you will never see your daughter again." Sean put the pen down and smiled at her.

"Are you serious?" Jessica said shaking her head. "My parents don't have that type of money."

"Oh, you'd be surprised what money your father really has," Sean told her. "I've done my research."

"You said you weren't going to hurt me."

"Yes, but they don't know that." Sean winked at her again.

"You cannot get away with this. There will be undercover agents hiding everywhere. You will get caught."

"Hmm." He scratched his bearded chin as if in deep thought. "Yes, we might have to find a good way to make the switch."

"You are still going to get caught. The bad people always get caught."

"I'm not bad," Sean reassured her. "I'm having fun. To be honest with you, I don't need the money; it's just all about the challenge of the job."

"I can think of other ways to have fun without taking other people's money." Jessica wiggled in her chair. He was entertained by her nervousness.

"But that's what makes it fun," Sean said leaning forward on the desk, "taking something that is not yours."

"I don't believe that. You are going to get caught."

"Help me to not get caught," Sean said staring deeply into her sparkling eyes.

"What? Why would I do that?"

"I want to see how smart you are." He grinned as he leaned back into his chair. "Pretend this is a game. How would you do it?"

Jessica took a deep breath and shook her head.

"Even though you tell them no cops, you know there will be some. There are always cops, just watch the movies."

"Okay, I figured that."

"Umm," she thought some more. "Maybe make the exchange in a crowded area."

"The cops would be in the crowd. You know, there will be some undercover."

"Have my mom leave the money and go."

"Someone will be watching the drop off." Sean was having fun with this.

"Let me pick up the money and deliver it to you. They won't arrest me," Jessica said putting her hands against the temples of her head and rubbed.

"You would have to check for a tracker in the money," he said. "They will most likely put one in there."

"I'd have to lead them on a wild goose chase or something."

"How?" He was really encouraging her to think.

"Drop the money down some hole in the ground like where city maintenance workers work. That hole leads to somewhere.

You guys be there waiting for the drop then take off. Or, I somehow make a switch and throw them off by leading them in a different route and drop the money somewhere so you guys can get it and go."

Sean smiled big. "Now that is thinking! Let's make it work!"

"Seriously?" Jessica looked surprised.

"Yes," he said. "It sounds good."

"I cannot do that." Jessica shook her head. "This is totally insane."

"Sure you can," Sean said. "If it doesn't look safe as we get into it, I will abort the job."

"You are going to get caught."

"No, because you are going to make sure we don't," he told her.

"Why would I do that?" Jessica asked.

"Because, I can feel that secretly you are excited about this and are curious to see if it will really work." Sean studied her face. "Besides, I think you like being here. You get to have a break from your hum drum life and now you can do whatever you want to do here…within reason, of course."

"I don't like being here," Jessica quickly replied. "I want to go home."

"So, this afternoon was all a lie. You are a good actress." He picked up the piece of paper and began folding it. "Help me and I will help you."

"If I don't?" Jessica asked bravely.

"Do you want me to hurt you?" Sean threatened. He knew he wouldn't but she didn't know that.

"You said you w-wouldn't." Jessica's voice trembled a bit.

"I could just keep you here until you give in and agree to help. I could lock you in your room and not let you out until you agree to help us."

"Fine." Jessica took a deep breath and stood up. "Lock me in the room."

That wasn't what Sean thought she'd say.

SEVEN

Jessica's hands were trembling. She never argued with someone before who had authority over her. But there was no way she was going to help them. This was insane. The look on Sean's face was that of surprise.

"Very well." Sean stood up. He pointed to the door. "You know the way to your room."

Jessica stomped out of the office like an angry teenager who didn't get her way. Bruce was still engrossed in the football game. Sean was walking a few steps behind her. She eyed the front door. She could make a run for it. She could push the lamp off the table as she ran by slowing Sean down and that might give her enough time to open the door and run to the neighbors for help. Her heart beat quickly as the adrenaline started building up inside her.

She took a quick breath and then did exactly as she planned. With adrenaline flowing through her body, she sprinted towards the door, pushing the lamp off the table as she passed by. She heard the lamp shatter as it hit the ground. She could hear Sean's heavy footsteps behind her. Just as she reached the doorknob Sean was right there pulling her away. His strong arms wrapped her in a good lock hold around her body and pulled her away from the door. She screamed loud and began struggling to get out of his arms. The more she struggled the tighter he held on to her.

"Let me go!" Jessica screamed as she squirmed in Sean's arms.

Bruce quickly jumped from his seat and went for the duct tape that was on the shelf.

"Stop it, Jess," Sean said holding her tightly in his arms. Jessica finally relaxed a little and stopped struggling.

Bruce ripped off a piece of duct tape and was heading over to put it over her mouth.

"No," Sean said to Bruce. "She needed to try."

Jessica's breathing was heavy from her failed attempt. She stopped screaming and struggling and her anger was now replaced with tears. He loosened his hold around her and moved her back to the door and unlocked the door and opened it wide enough for her to look outside.

"Look," he told her. "Jess, look outside."

Jessica turned her face to peer out the door. The sun had already set so the sky was darkening. Tall trees surrounded this large property. There was no neighbor in sight. The driveway to the house meshed with a dirt road that led towards some tall trees that looked like it headed to a main road somewhere. This house was on a secluded piece of land.

"No one would have heard you," he said softly in her ear. "You have nowhere to run to because you don't know where we are."

Jessica didn't stop the tears this time. She let them flow and she turned and buried her face in his chest as she cried. His arms that were once tight around her loosened, and now he was holding her in a soothing and comforting way. He stroked her hair as he held her close to his chest.

"Come on," he said softly, "Let's take you to your room to calm down and think."

Sean followed her up the stairs and she wiped her wet eyes. Once to the room she ran right for the bed, flopping down and hugging the pillow while she let out a few more tears. Sean closed the door. She could hear the lock go back on the door.

Sean was the one who held the cards here. If she kept acting like a silly child and being defiant, he would just keep her here. At this point, if they would just let her go, she promised herself she wouldn't tell the cops anything. She just wanted to be home and get back to her quiet life.

Jessica eventually stopped crying. She lay on her back looking up at the ceiling. Her feelings had changed again and now she felt vengeful. *I could make his life a living hell every day I'm here*, she smiled at that thought, but then again, if she just did as he said, she could get out of here by Wednesday. That was actually the only thing she really could do.

She changed her mind again. No, she was going to tell the cops everything when she got home. She has seen their faces and she knew their names. They would be punished for everything they had done to her. But the one thing that confused her was Sean knew that, so why had they left that as a way to get caught? Did he want to get caught?

As time slowly passed, the room grew darker. The sun had retired completely from the sky. Jessica didn't want to get up and turn on the light. The best thing to do was just lie there in darkness until she fell asleep. She kicked off her shoes. This was not how she wanted to spend this weekend. "I will never go down an alley again." Jessica mumbled aloud. Her eyes were getting heavy now. Boredom had taken over. If only she had her book, she could escape into their world. Her eyes fluttered closed.

Her mind recalled the afternoon today. It was fun. More fun than she had had since being in high school with one of her friends. Connie really did make her look good. Best of all, she felt better about the way she looked. Then, there was that awkward moment when Sean grabbed her arm and twirled her around as they were dancing. His closeness to her made her heart flutter with excitement as he placed her hands around his neck, and he put his on her waist. His chocolate dark eyes looked deep into her soul. Why was it so easy to talk to him? She could not even say a word to Trent, but she managed to have a long conversation with Sean. Her mind wandered to this morning where he stood there trimming his beard while his shirt was unbuttoned. He looked extremely sexy. Why did he have to be the bad man?

Jessica felt her body get warmer and then she felt her glasses being removed from her face. She quickly opened her eyes. Sean had taken her glasses off and was putting them on the nightstand. A blanket was pulled over the top of her. He turned back and looked at her and took his hand and wiped the hair out of her face very gently.

"I'm sorry," he said softly. "I shouldn't make you do this."

"I shouldn't have tried to run," Jessica whispered. "That was stupid of me."

"I would have tried if I were in your situation," he said with a smile. "I don't blame you for trying."

Jessica's eyes wandered from his face to his chest. His shirt was unbuttoned all the way like this morning. Her heart beat a little quicker as she admired his strong looking chest in the shadows.

He reached across to the night stand and lifted a glass.

"Water?" He offered the glass to her. "I thought you'd be thirsty. You've been up here for a few hours."

"I have nowhere to go." Jessica sat up in bed. Jessica reached out and took the glass from Sean. Their fingers touched briefly which made her stomach do a quick flip flop. He sat on the edge of the bed by her.

"Funny," he said, "I was thinking about what Connie had said earlier about you and your so- called boyfriend and didn't you say you have issues making conversation?"

"Yes." Jessica nodded.

"You are talking to me just fine," he told me. "Why is that?"

"I don't know," Jessica replied after her sip of water. "You are older, I guess."

"I'm not that much older than you. I think you just need to push yourself, be brave, and talk to him. Find something to talk about and that would break the tension between you two."

"He has a girlfriend, I'm sure of it."

"You can win him over, I guarantee it."

There was silence. Jessica tried to pull her eyes away from his sexy body.

"Why have you revealed your faces and names to me?" Jessica asked. "Aren't you afraid I will turn you in?"

"I'm hoping you won't," he replied. "We haven't hurt you. Remember, we just want to be thieves and take money, we aren't kidnappers."

He was right. She was confused about what she should do.

"What time is Connie going to be here in the morning?" Jessica changed the subject.

"Hopefully by 8:00. If she isn't here, I will stick around until she does get here."

"What about your job?" Jessica wondered. "Most people would get in trouble for showing up late to work, especially on a Monday."

"I'm in control of what I do." He smiled. "I set my hours, for the most part."

"Are you going to let me call my parents?"

"You need to sound distraught when you call," he said. "You seem pretty calm right now. I've sent Bruce off with the letter to have it delivered. They will get it soon. I'm sure they are going to want proof of life, so maybe we will try and call tomorrow, briefly."

"Thank you," Jessica said as she handed the glass of water back to Sean, "for not hurting me yet."

He smiled that adorable smile again.

"I've never had any plans on hurting you." He stood up. "I'm not that kind of bad guy."

Jessica laughed.

"Sorry I called you a bad guy. You just have different views of what's right, I guess."

"Go to sleep, Jess," he said. "I'm not locking this door, just to let you know. However, there is an alarm on the front and back door that would have to be deactivated before you can go out. You don't know the code. Oh, and there is no house phone, only my cell phone. Don't go anywhere, okay. I've enjoyed you being here."

"I'm not going anywhere. Nowhere to go." Jessica scooted back down on the bed. "I promise I won't leave."

"If you need anything," he said. "I'm just in the next room."

She nodded.

"Good night," he said as he walked away. He closed the door. She didn't hear any locks.

When he left the room, she got out of her clothes and into that nightgown that Connie gave her yesterday. It was a pink silky gown that hung to just about her knees; probably something that Connie would be wearing as she tried to seduce Sean.

Her talk with Sean woke her up. Falling asleep was going to be hard now. The thought then went through her mind; she was alone in the house with Sean. Connie and Bruce were gone. She'd never been alone with a guy before like this, even if he was in another room.

The vision of Sean with his shirt open kept running through her mind. She imagined her hands touching his chest. He did hold her in his arms, sort of. He had strong arms. He did smell good; that was for certain. That had been the closest she'd ever been to a man that wasn't her father. It was exciting, now that she was thinking about it. She smiled as she let her mind wander to many possibilities. After all, a girl can dream.

****

After Sean had left Jessica earlier when she tried to escape, he began to really feel terrible for making her cry. He didn't want to be the bad guy. He typed up the ransom note on the computer and printed it out. Being very carefully to not put fingerprints on the paper or envelope, he sealed it and handed it off to Bruce and asked him to go deliver it and go home.

He couldn't keep his mind off Jessica. Maybe it was fate that she showed up; fate for his lonely heart. He didn't want to think romantic thoughts about her, but it was hard not to when she looked so pretty. Even if Connie didn't straighten her hair, he still thought she was pretty. It was bad timing for fate, though. He had a job to do and he needed to do it quickly. This was dragging out longer than he wanted.

After a few hours of silence upstairs, he went up to check on Jessica. She was curled up on her side hugging the extra pillow. Her eyes were closed, and she looked as though she was cold. She must have fallen asleep. He picked up the Afghan that was lying at the foot of the bed and carefully draped it over her. It wasn't until he reached over and took her glasses off that she woke up. They had a nice conversation and even though it was dark in the room, he could tell she was eyeing his physique. He wondered what was going through her mind.

Maybe if she felt like he trusted her she wouldn't turn them in. That is why he left the door unlocked. When he left her room, he wandered to his room and changed into his sleepwear which consisted of black sleep pants. He went back downstairs to his office to send a private message on his other cell phone explaining the conversation he had with Victor. He hated living this double life. He was really hoping he could find the Midnight Star and end this for good.

He wasn't sure how long he was staring at some plans on his desk before his eyes couldn't stay open any longer. He folded his arms on the desk and put his head down. He'd just rest his eyes for a few minutes then he'd clean up and go to bed.

In his dream he was holding Jessica in his arms and dancing slow with her. She smelled so good and her skin was so soft. As he touched her lips with his it was so warm, and it made his heart race. He felt a nudge on his bare back. His dream turned to Connie and her nudging him. It irritated him. He didn't like her at all, yet he had to lead her on. His hopes would be that she could share some secrets as to where Victor would have hidden the diamond. After all, she knew him more than he did.

He felt a harder nudge on his back, and he lifted his head wearily from his hands.

"What do you want, Connie?" He grumbled.

"You shouldn't sleep in here." Jessica's sweet voice filled his ears. "It's not comfortable."

He turned his eyes up to her and smiled. "Oh, Jess, it's you." He stretched. "I was comfortable. Is it morning already?" He picked up his watch to look at it.

"N-n-no," Jessica stuttered nervously as her eyes roamed over his bare chest. His heart quickened a bit knowing she liked what she saw.

His eyes focused on her and what she was wearing. It was one of Connie's nightgowns. She looked extremely sexy. The silky fabric hugged her shape very well, much better than when Connie wore it. He could see her chest rise quicker as he gazed over her body.

"What are you doing up?" He asked.

"Um-I'm h-hungry," Jessica managed to say. "Chinese food makes me hungry after a few hours."

Sean stood up. Her eyes continued gazing at his bare chest. The sides of his lips turned up into a grin.

"I'm hungry, too," he said. He walked past her, almost touching her arm. Jessica turned off the light to the office as they exited the room.

Sean walked ahead and flipped on the light in the kitchen. Jessica paused by the garbage can where the pieces to the broken lamp were tossed.

"Sorry about the lamp," she said with sadness in her voice.

"No worries. I didn't like that lamp anyway." He opened the fridge. "So, what were you planning on eating?"

"Not quite sure, you don't have much food in your fridge."

"I'm not used to visitors." He smiled at her.

"I did see some jam in there…maybe PB and J sandwich?" Jessica suggested. "I live on my own, too. That's always a good fall back item."

He pulled out the grape jelly and the milk. He opened the lid and gave it a sniff to make sure it was good. She walked past him and pulled the bread and the peanut butter from the cupboard. Sean reached for a butter knife and began preparing the sandwiches. While he was spreading the peanut butter, some got on his finger. He began to raise it to his mouth to lick it off and then in an instant, he changed his mind.

Jessica was leaning up against the counter pouring their milk. He moved his finger over to her mouth. She just stood there with a scared look on her face, not knowing what to do.

"Open your mouth," he insisted in a deep seductive voice.

Jessica slowly opened her mouth and he placed the tip of his finger inside her mouth with the peanut butter on it. She closed her lips to pull the peanut butter from his finger. Warmth flowed over his body. He shouldn't have done that.

Her cheeks reddened. He withdrew his hand from her lips and then he put a little more on his finger then licked it off, keeping eye contact with her. He guessed the dreams he had of her was encouraging him to make it real.

He handed her the plate with the sandwich on it. She took it quickly then sat down at the table not looking at him. He shook his head without her seeing. He shouldn't have done that. She was probably scared to death of him now.

EIGHT

Jessica's heart was beating way too fast. That was just too exciting. She'd read things like that in her novels but to actually experience it was so…dare she say wonderful. She couldn't look at him. She shouldn't be here, wearing this silky nightgown without a robe in front of him. He was her captor. She shouldn't have these types of feelings for him.

Sean sat down at the table with her. He brought the cups of milk to the table since she forgot them after that hot scene. She sat looking at her sandwich and reliving his finger in her mouth.

"Aren't you hungry?" He questioned.

"Umm," Jessica started to stutter again but a little more than usual. "Y-yes. I just…well, wow." She still didn't look at him, but from the corner of her eye, she could see him smiling. She picked up her sandwich and took a bite. It was hard to focus on eating with this type of tension between them.

"Do you always look this good when you go to sleep?" He flirted.

"These aren't my clothes," she quickly said. "It's all that was there. I don't sleep in things like this."

"What do you sleep in?"

"Nothing fancy, shorts and a tee-shirt." She took another small bite. "Nothing sleazy like this."

"I happen to like sleazy," he said with a tease in his voice.

Jessica's face began to tingle, and she could feel her face growing warm again. This was an awkward conversation. She quickly shoved more of the sandwich in her mouth to hurry and finish so she could go back to the bedroom where it was safer. She washed it down with milk.

"Maybe I'd better lock my door tonight," she found herself saying out loud.

Sean laughed. "Yes, you might have to."

She finished her milk pretending she didn't hear his remarks. Why was he flirting with her? This was so not right. He was playing with her thoughts right now and that was not safe.

"I think I'm done now." Jessica said quickly. She fumbled with the napkin, wiped her mouth and stood up. Her heart continued to beat uncontrollably. "Th-thank you for the sandwich. I-I think I will go to bed now."

"Am I making you nervous?" He asked knowing darn right that he was.

Jessica took a step then paused. "Goodnight, Sean." She turned to walk away but he reached out and took her arm gently, stopping her.

"Not yet," he said keeping her from walking away. He moved her closer to him as he stood up. She could feel her heart beating so fast she thought it would burst from her chest. He took her trembling hand and placed it on his chest. Jessica stiffened up and a slight sigh escaped her throat, without permission. He was warm.

"I know you've wanted to do this, Jess," Sean said. "So, do it."

Jessica could feel her face growing hot and it probably shone bright like Rudolph's nose. His skin under her hand was smooth and her hand began trembling, but she did as her heart and mind had wanted to do. She slightly moved her fingers and then her whole hand over his chest. He had a tiny bit of hair on his chest and she moved her hand up further. He took a hold of her other hand and brought it to his chest as well. Jessica couldn't look in his eyes. She kept her eyes focused on his chest as she let both hands wander over his warm skin. She could feel his heart beating quickly, too.

A panic flag flew up in her mind. What was she doing? This could not be right, but if felt so right. She gulped hard.

"I've got to go to bed," Jessica said quickly as the warning bell sounded like Big Ben in her head.

She took her hands off of his chest. Without looking at him she hurried out of the kitchen and ran to her room.

****

When Jessica opened her eyes, there was light coming in from the little window announcing that it was morning. It took her a moment to gain her thoughts as to where she was and what happened last night. She felt an overwhelming guilty feeling. She allowed herself to put her hands on Sean's chest and move her hands across his skin. Connie was going to kill her!

Maybe it was a dream. Yes, it was a dream, Jessica convinced herself. She rolled out of bed and grabbed the afghan around her since she had no bathrobe. She needed to go to the bathroom. Her door was still unlocked, thankfully, so she opened the door and quickly made it across the hallway to the bathroom. Her makeup had smeared under her eyes from sleep. She washed her face and then rinsed her mouth out as well since it still lingered of peanut butter. She grabbed the brush and ran it through her hair that was now starting to curl up again. She was sure her clothes were dry. Maybe it was best she wore her own clothes today.

Jessica opened the door to the bathroom and stepped out and right into the pathway of Sean. Once again, he had a very nice dress shirt on with a tie just hanging around his neck. His shirt was not buttoned. He smelled clean and his brown hair looked damp from his shower.

"Good morning," he said as he gazed over her. "Sleep well?"

"I...I suppose," Jessica stuttered nervously and tried not to look at him. "Is Connie here?"

"No, not yet. She had too much to drink last night and she crashed at her apartment," he said. "She said that she'd come over at 9:00 or so."

Jessica stepped out of the doorway of the bathroom to let him go in. She pulled the blanket around tighter to hide her body.

"I'm sorry if I made you feel uncomfortable last night," Sean said as he reached for his electric razor. He turned it on and started running it over his neck. "I shouldn't have done that."

"I..I.." she didn't know what to say except stutter like an idiot. "I've never done that before."

"I could tell," he said as he lifted his chin to run the razor under it. "That is one thing you will need to get comfortable with if you are going to make your move on that guy at work."

"Oh, I doubt I'll be touching his chest," Jessica blurted out.

"You never know," he turned off his razor and ran his hands over his face to check for any stubble. "One thing usually leads to another." He splashed on some cologne and then started buttoning up his shirt. "Can you tie a tie?" He asked her.

"I did once for my father, years ago," she said. "It was pretty sloppy."

"Come here," he said motioning for her to join him in the bathroom. "I'll show you."

"Why?" Jessica nervously asked. "That is a guy's job."

"But it is so much fun to have your girl tie your tie," he said with a smile. "I'll teach you."

Jessica slowly walked to where he was standing and stopped in front of him. Was he referring to her as 'his girl?' Maybe her mind was playing tricks on her. He didn't mean it. No, he couldn't have. Oh, being this close to him, and smelling his freshly splashed on cologne made her heart race again. He smelled so good. He buttoned up his top button and then proceeded to show her the basic tie. It was hard to focus on instructions with him that close to her.

"Now you do it," he said.

With shaky hands she started to follow the steps on the tie. Her blanket had dropped to the ground since she couldn't hold onto it and tie the tie. Jessica could feel his minty breath on her face since they were closer than she wanted to be right now.

"It's messy," She said as she tried to straighten it. By doing so, her hands had rested on his chest again, but this time it was through his clothing. Tingles shot through her body again.

"You did fine." he winked at her. "I like it."

Jessica stepped back away from him taking her hands off him before she wanted to touch him more. He bent down and picked up her blanket and placed it around her shoulders. His hands lingered on her.

"I'll help you," Jessica finally said, "to not get caught."

"Why the change of heart?" He asked.

"I just think I'd better go soon. I'm stopping you and your team from doing whatever you do normally without a prisoner."

"You make it sound so final. A prisoner. You just happen to be a good bargaining chip right now."

"So, if money is all you want," Jessica said trying to step back again from him. "I'll do my best to get it for you."

"Money isn't everything if you cannot share it with others," he said as he took his hand and brushed the side of her face with it. "I'm not all about money. I can be a normal person, too."

"I'm sure my parents will have to take out a bunch of loans to get the $50,000. I'll move back in with them and my paycheck can pay them back," Jessica said sadly. "Maybe I'll go back to college and become something else."

"College? Good decision. What do you want to be?"

"Maybe interior design," Jessica told him.

"Good choice," he said. "You brighten any room with just your presence."

What is he doing? Jessica thought. His words were confusing her for sure.

"Umm, okay. If you say so." Her mouth was drying up.

"Oh, I do," he said stepping a little closer to her. "Jess, you are very beautiful. Don't sell yourself short." His hands went back to her cheek as he took his knuckles and rubbed them gently on her cheeks.

"I'm standing here with no makeup on my face and you are shooting me compliments? Did you get enough sleep last night?"

"Actually, no, I didn't get enough sleep last night." He smiled. "You kind of left me a little flustered last night and thoughts of you were in my head."

"I-I did?" her nervous stutter started again.

"Yes," he said as he took his hands and ran them down her arms and then took a hold of her hands that were clutching the blanket around her. "I think you are correct to say that it is time for you to go. But I'm selfish, right now, and I don't want you to go." He brought her hands up to his lips and kissed them gently.

Jessica could feel her face growing warm. Butterflies danced in her belly. She sucked in a deep breath. Her whole body was warm but trembled from excitement.

"But, Connie.." Jessica started to say.

"I like you, Jess," he said. "We can leave Connie out of this."

He took her hands and placed them on his chest again. Her blanket dropped again from her shoulders. She wanted to move away but her feet wouldn't move like they were glued to the floor. This was completely wrong, but it felt so right. Her hands moved slowly across his chest with his hands on top of hers. She could get use to this feeling.

****

Sean wasn't quite sure what he was doing. When Jessica was around him, he seemed to do things a different way. He felt like a schoolboy. Jessica looked so beautiful this morning that he couldn't control the thoughts that were going through his mind. He wanted to pick her up and carry her back to his room and kiss her passionately. He was shocked at the way she was responding to him as he encouraged her to touch his chest. He didn't want her touching another man, he wanted her touching him.

He pulled her closer to him so he could keep his hands on her waist and back. He moved his hands in circular motion across her lower back. Her hands remained on his chest. Now he wished he hadn't buttoned his shirt up. He loved it when she had her hands on him last night. It sent chills over his body. He hadn't felt like that with other women. When he kissed her hands a moment ago, he could see the passion in her eyes, as well.

His phone began ringing in his room. He heard a sigh escape her mouth. He didn't move away from her. He kept his gaze on her. The phone rang again. He looked down at her lips then back to her eyes. The phone rang a third time.

"You'd better get that," Jessica broke the silence. Her voice had a slight tremble to it.

Sean smiled a little then moved away from her and went to his room to answer his phone. He was irritated with the person who called. He almost kissed her.

"Sean," the person on the other end said. "I found a good quick job to do tonight."

"Jack," Sean said. "Things are a little complicated with Jess here."

"Jess?" Jack asked. "Who's that?"

"The lady you, Connie and Bruce grabbed Saturday."

"Oh, she's still there?"

"Yeah." Sean paused. "Does the job look safe?"

"As safe as any other one. Swing by and get the plans from me today. It has to be done tonight, otherwise the shipment moves."

Sean walked back into the hallway with his phone to his ear. Jessica was gone. She was back in her room with the door closed. He sighed quietly.

"Fine, what time?" Sean asked.

"Meet at ten." Jack told him. "Victor doesn't know about this job. I figured we need our own cut. He's too slow to deliver our money."

"Agreed. Ten it is. I'll see you tonight." Sean hung up the phone.

It seemed that now members of this team were not agreeing with Victor's leadership. He needed to step up the game tomorrow with Victor. He would go to Victor's house to search for the diamond.

Sean glanced at his watch. Now that the mood was shot, he needed to think of something else. Food. Yes, food was a good distraction. Even though he badly wanted to kiss Jessica's lips, he also didn't want the distraction of her being here. He stood by her door then knocked.

"Jess, get dressed, let's get some breakfast," he said then hurried downstairs without her reply.

****

Jessica sat on the edge of the bed staring off into space. She kept feeling the warmth of Sean's touch as he held her in his arms. He was going to kiss her, she knew it. What scared her most about this was she was going to let him. *Oh, this is so bad*, she thought. She needed to make sure they weren't alone like that ever again. He was her captor, not her lover. Guys like him were bad luck indeed.

Jessica quickly got dressed with some extra clothes she found in the drawer that was most likely Connie's. The Levi's didn't have cuts in them, just plain tight Levi's. A black t-shirt with some logo printed on it was quickly pulled over her head. Now she didn't look tempting. She fluffed her hair and applied some make up that wasn't as much as what Connie put on her.

Within ten minutes she stood at the top of the stairs looking down. Her heart was still beating fast as she wasn't looking forward to seeing Sean again after their intense romantic moment. She took a deep breath then walked down the stairs. Sean was in the kitchen with his phone in his hand typing something.

"W-what's for breakfast?" Jessica asked in a shaky voice.

He looked up at her and his eyes wandered over her wardrobe choice and smiled.

"Well, since there isn't anything here, we are going out," he said as he handed her a black beanie hat and the blindfold.

"We are leaving the house?" Jessica panicked.

"Yes, we are." He also handed her an oversized jacket. "Put this on, too."

Jessica did as instructed. He took a hold of her hand and her heart sped up. He pulled her gently and she began walking keeping the other hand out in front of her so she wouldn't bump into anything. She heard the door open and a security code being entered then the door closed. The temperature changed around her, feeling cooler. It was the middle of September, but Winslow wasn't this cool. They must be closer to the mountains.

A car door opened, and Sean carefully maneuvered her around into the seat. She sat a little lower in the car so the car must be a sports car. She felt his hand move across her body as he put the buckle in its place. She could smell his cologne and it made her remember the moment they had earlier. She sucked in a breath and quickly entwined her fingers together on her lap to keep from grabbing him and pulling him in for a kiss.

The door closed and he soon entered on the driver's side and started the vehicle. She heard the garage door rise and then he backed out.

"Won't people think it weird with you driving me wearing a blindfold?" Jessica asked nervously.

"Once I get far enough away from my home, I will let you take it off. I just need to have you not see where I live."

"Since I know you live in a secluded spot, did you choose this because you don't like neighbors?" She asked him.

"I don't need nosey neighbors. So, I prefer an out of the way area."

Jessica paid attention to the movements of the car as it drove straight for bit, made a left turn, then a few moments later another right. Then a left....Was that a right or left? Jessica thought to herself. She was trying to make a mental note of how to get to his house.

"You can take the blindfold off, but leave the beanie on," Sean said.

She pulled off the blindfold and quickly looked around. They were in a small town with small stores lining the street. *Where were they?* She thought.

"How far away from my home are we?" Jessica asked.

"A ways." Was his reply.

"So, am I recognizable here?"

"Sure, your picture is up everywhere. You are a celebrity. However, they are looking for a young lady with really curly brown hair and glasses. You don't look like that."

"Oh," she said. "I wonder what picture they used."

"It looked a little outdated. I suppose your folks still think of you as a high school kid."

He started to slow down as a fast food establishment was nearing.

"We are going to go through the drive-thru and order breakfast biscuits. Is that okay with you?"

"Yes, that's fine," Jessica said.

"I want you to look out your window as we are in the drive-thru. Do not make eye contact with anyone."

Jessica nodded and obeyed as Sean placed their order. She looked around the town to see if there was anything that would give their location away. Nothing. The town wasn't that busy, so it was a small town. The mountains were close by, but there were many towns around Winslow that were located at the foot of the mountains.

As they waited for their food, she tried to make small talk.

"Did you buy this car with the money you stole?"

"No," he replied. "I bought this honestly."

"What made you want to rob jewelry stores and banks?"

"Not sure, it just happened one day," he said looking away. "I know security systems. That makes me valuable to Victor."

"Did you take the Midnight Star necklace?" Jessica asked bluntly.

"No, Victor did."

The lady in the drive-thru handed their purchase thru the window. He thanked her and pulled away handing the bag to Jessica.

"How did he do it?" Jessica asked. "The newspapers say they have no clue."

"I wasn't with him when he took it," Sean admitted.

Jessica stayed quiet as they drove through town slowly.

"Who was on the phone earlier?" she asked breaking the silence again.

"You are full of questions, aren't you?" Sean laughed.

"I don't like silence."

"It was another guy in the group. He was the one who was driving the van when Bruce and Connie grabbed you."

"What did he want?"

"He found us another job to do tonight. He was asking to see if I wanted in."

"A-are you going to do it?" Jessica asked with a stutter.

"Sure." He smiled at her. "Why not?"

"Well, it's tonight. You will have to get rid of me first."

"Actually," he said took another glance at her, "I was thinking of bringing you along."

Jessica could feel the color from her face drain. Her heart beat fast as anxiety filled her body.

"What?" she gasped. "No, that's not a good thing!"

NINE

Sean noticed how nervous Jessica got when he suggested bringing her with them.

"We have to do it tonight," he told her. "It's the only window of opportunity and we have to have all four of us there. I cannot leave you alone in the house."

"Just lock me in the closet," she practically cried. "I don't want to go!"

"Besides, we will need another lookout," he said. "That's all you have to do is watch for cops."

"I'm not a professional! I cannot do that."

"If I can think of somewhere else to put you, I will." He stopped at a stop light. "But for now, you are coming with us. It will be fun. Put the blindfold back on please."

With shaky hands she put the blindfold back on. The light turned green and he began the winding and twisting route back to his secluded hideaway. He really didn't want to involve Jessica in the heist, but he knew he couldn't leave her alone. The only solution was to bring her along.

He pulled into the garage and turned off the engine. He got out and helped her out of the car. He led her with one hand while she still held onto their breakfast. He released the alarm on his house and they walked inside.

"You can take the blindfold off," Sean said as he closed the door.

Jessica removed the blindfold and replaced it with her glasses that were sitting on the table. She sat down pulling out their food.

"There has to be another way," she said bringing up the heist again.

"I will think about it while I'm at work," he said. "What I want you to do is work on that plan of yours and how to lead the police in a different direction, so we don't get caught."

"I doubt it will be a good plan," she said taking a bite of her breakfast sandwich.

"You will do a spectacular job, I just know it." He opened up his breakfast sandwich. "I was thinking that while we are out tonight, we better call your folks."

"The police will trace the phone to your city!" Jessica's voice got excited. She actually seemed a little worried.

"The job is not in my city. We don't rob from my city."

"Did my parents get the ransom note?" Jessica asked.

"Yes, they did last night. Bruce dropped it off." He put down his biscuit. "You know, you need to sound distraught when you call. You know, scared, frightened, and crying. Do you think you can do that? I just don't think you sound very convincing lately."

"I will try to be upset when I call," she said casually.

"Be a bit more convincing, okay?"

"You have taken good care of me. I guess I am really lucky."

"Yes, I think you are very lucky it was us who kidnapped you. We aren't very good kidnappers." He chuckled.

"No, you aren't. You are nothing like the movies or books that I have read," She said as she smiled. He liked it when she smiled. She had a little dimple in her left cheek. "I feel like I've been taken by a bunch of friends on a trip somewhere."

"A bunch of friends, huh?" He questioned as he bunched up the wrapper of his biscuit.

"Everyone needs friends," Jessica said. "Even if they are thieves."

Sean grew quiet for a moment then he said sadly,

"Huh, I was hoping we were a little more than friends after last night."

He could see her swallow hard. He enjoyed seeing her fidget in her seat.

"Umm...I..."she started stuttering again. "You are my friend."

"So, do you touch all your guy friends like that?"

"I don't touch my friends like that..." she quickly said. "You made me do it."

"Oh, blame it on me, huh?" he smiled and took a drink. "You know, you didn't have to stay. You could have turned and went to bed."

"What would you have done if you were in my situation?" Jessica quickly asked.

"Well, if I had a beautiful lady standing in front of me telling me to touch her, I would."

"You are a man. That's a normal reaction."

"And yours was not?"

"I don't know, Sean," Jessica paused. "I've never done that before. I've never had that opportunity. So, I suppose I am like you. I had a handsome man standing in front of me telling me to touch him, so I guess I have to."

Sean smiled.

"There, that wasn't so hard was it?" he asked. "Admitting what you want."

"So, if I see a handsome guy I should just go up and say I want to touch your chest?"

"Sure, why not?" he laughed. "You know, I can help you with this boyfriend you are stalking at work."

"I'm not stalking him." She paused. "Well, maybe just a little. But, what do you mean?"

"Well, for one thing," he said, "you have been talking and making good conversations with me, so if anything, I might make it easier for you to talk to this guy."

"But I get nervous when I talk. I stutter."

"I think it's cute," he smiled and sent her a wink. "Guys like it when girls are nervous around them. It makes them feel more confident."

"But I might say the wrong thing," Jessica said. "I don't want to look stupid."

"You haven't said anything wrong yet with me. Connie has shown you how to style your hair differently and given you different clothes to wear to make you more attractive than you already are. Personally, I don't think you need to change anything." He paused a moment and took another sip of his drink. "Pick your clothes wisely. Have them accentuate your hips, your butt, your neck and your breasts." His eyes wandered over her body as he said those words.

Immediately Jessica's cheeks grew pink from embarrassment. She looked away from him. He reached for her hand. "And, it's okay to blush, too. Another thing guys like. It gives away your feelings."

"It's not fair, guys don't blush," Jessica said as she began fanning her face to cool it off with her other hand that wasn't being held by his.

"Oh, we do," Sean admitted. "We just don't do it as easily as girls do." He paused a moment. "I've worked with you on closeness. You are doing very well with that."

"Closeness?" Jessica asked.

"Tie my tie," he said as he reminded her of their closeness this morning. "I'm trying to make you feel comfortable around guys."

"Okay, so I get it now," Jessica yanked her hand away from Sean's. She pushed the food away from her. "I am very naïve." She stood up. "I am inexperienced, I know that, and I now know what you are doing. You are just playing with my emotions." She picked up her wrapper and tossed it in the garbage can. He could see she was very irritated. "I'm another job for you. Something for you to conquer." She shook her head. "I cannot believe that I was falling for this."

Sean didn't expect Jessica to retaliate like this. He stood up and reached for her arm and grabbed a hold of it so she wouldn't walk away. He pulled her closer to him. She struggled a little. He put both his arms around her. She kept her eyes downward.

"Look at me," Sean said.

Jessica lifted her gaze to his. He looked into her dark blue eyes. He could get lost in those eyes so easily.

"You are not a job for me," he said. "I do like you. Since the moment you were brought into this house, I've needed to protect you. You are not safe here. Not safe with Victor. But now, I've realized you aren't completely safe with me either, because every time I see you, I want to hold you in my arms and kiss you."

He leaned down and put his lips on hers and softly kissed them. Jessica stiffened up but soon she relaxed in his arms and melted into him. He pulled her even closer to him as his mouth wandered over hers and she eagerly kissed him back. He could tell that she was enjoying this as much as he was. She moved her hands up his chest and touched his neck then his hair. He pulled away briefly to look her in her eyes again.

"I'm not playing you, I promise." His voice was soft. He kissed her again. "And I will protect you."

"How can you protect me from you?" Jessica grinned as she kissed his neck.

"By getting you out of here safely," he said as he stepped back. "You cannot be here."

"Then just let me go," she said. "I promise I won't tell anyone who you are." She moved her hands over his chest again and tingles fell over his body. He leaned in and trapped her lips with his.

"I don't want to let you go," he whispered as he continued to kiss her as he backed her up against the wall.

The sound of the garage door opening quickly ended their romantic moment. Jessica's breaths were heavy, and her lips were puffy.

"Connie is here," he whispered.

"Oh, she's going to kill me." Jessica backed away. He kept a hold of her hands.

"No, she won't." He winked at her. "She will kill me."

Jessica pulled completely away and quickly ran upstairs to her room. Sean smiled as he relived the memory of her lips on his. She wanted the kiss just as badly as he did. He began cleaning up the table as Connie entered the home. In her arms was a bag of groceries.

"Since you don't shop," she said putting the groceries on the table, "I took the liberty of getting stuff for us for lunch and dinner tonight."

"Thank you," he said looking at his watch to see the time. "Okay, Jess is upstairs. She has homework to do and she's going to need your expertise. She needs to come up with a plan for the exchange of her and money without getting us caught."

"What?" Connie gasped. "You are going to leave that to her to think about? She can't do that."

"That's why you are here." Sean touched her face gently. "And, we have a job tonight."

"Oh sweet! But, what about Jessica?"

"She's coming with." Sean headed to the back door. "It will be fun." Sean walked out the door.

TEN

Jessica sat on the edge of the bed again. She couldn't get the grin off her face. Her first kiss was magical and wonderful. Oh, his lips were so soft. She touched her lips again. Her stomach had butterflies dancing inside of it. Sean was amazing. She sighed. This was so good.

Reality slapped her out of her love thoughts.

"Sean is the bad guy," Jessica said softly to herself. "I'm going to be gone soon and I'll never see him again."

She fell back onto the bed. This is so bad.

"I'll just stay away from him," she whispered to herself. "Yes, that's what will happen. If I have to stay locked in my room until he leaves each day then so be it."

After Jessica heard the back door close and the sound of Sean's car leaving, she gave herself some moments alone then she went downstairs, hoping Connie couldn't tell what happened. Connie was putting away the groceries when she stepped into the kitchen.

"Oh, there you are," Connie said closing the door. "Sean says we have some work to do."

"Yes, we need to come up with a plan to not get everyone caught in the exchange."

"Let me go get some paper out of Sean's office." Connie hurried by Jessica and then stopped outside of the office. "Um, did something happen last night?"

"W-what do you mean?" Jessica asked quickly with a stutter as she remembered the late-night peanut butter moment.

Connie studied Jessica a little more then turned and went into the office for some paper. Jessica sat down in the chair at the table feeling extremely guilty. Connie knew what happened; she just knew it.

"The lamp is missing," Connie said.

"Oh, that," Jessica laughed. "I tried to get away and broke the lamp in the process."

"I see it didn't work. Sorry."

Connie returned to the table with paper and a couple of pencils.

"Okay, where is this going to take place?" she asked.

"Winslow Mall," Jessica said. "There are a lot of places to wander around there, especially in the food court area."

"I'm going to need to go to the Mall and do a quick scope of everything later. Can you draw a quick sketch of the area?"

"Sure," Jessica said as she took the paper and started drawing out the place.

"So, your mom will give you the money, right?"

"Yes," Jessica nodded.

"There will be a tracker in the bag, most likely. You will need to switch bags. I'll buy some identical bags."

Jessica pushed over the sketch of the mall that she made and began to explain.

"There is a door right here, it's by the theater. When people exit the theater, they come out of this door into the food court and then there is this one door that leads to the outside, to an alley way that leads to the parking lot."

"That would be the perfect spot for the drop. Bruce can be out here as you toss the bag—"

"Or, I toss the bag that they think is the bag of money out the door, and everyone goes running to that area and I actually drop the money in the theater. Bruce can be in the theater and grab it from there."

Connie's eyes brightened. "We can have the drop off time right as an afternoon movie is letting out. People can come out and Bruce could look like a guy just leaving from a movie. He won't get caught!"

Jessica nodded. This plan just might work after all.

"I can lead them on a little tour around the shops through the food court to throw them off." She smiled big.

"Jessica, if I'm not mistaken, you sound like you are excited about this."

"I just want to go home," Jessica quickly said. "I just hope I still have a job to go to."

"I'm sure they will hold it for you. Besides, you need to strut your stuff around that guy."

"What guy?" she asked not thinking.

"The guy at your work that you like, um, Trent?"

"Oh, him." Jessica blushed. She had forgotten all about him. No one could compare to Sean.

"Jessica." Connie studied her real closely. "Sean kissed you, didn't he?"

Jessica's face started growing warm from the guilt. She looked down towards the paper.

"Oh, my gosh!" Connie gasped. "He did kiss you!"

"I didn't mean it to happen," she said, still not looking at Connie. "I'm so sorry." She closed her eyes waiting for Connie to possibly strike her or something. Nothing happened.

Connie laughed.

"He's a good kisser, isn't he?" she smiled as Jessica looked up.

"Um-yeah," she said blushing again. "But I don't have anyone to compare him to."

"There is no comparison," Connie said. "Sean is wonderful. I just wish there would have been more between us, but, he seemed more interested in becoming buddy-buddy with Victor."

"Why would he do that?" she asked. "Is it because of the jewelry and the money?"

"I personally think that Sean wants to be the lead man and get rid of Victor. I wouldn't be a bit surprised if he sets him up to get caught."

"Would Sean really do that?" she asked in shock.

"I think he wants the Midnight Star," Connie told her. "He wants it for himself. That necklace alone costs around three million dollars."

Jessica's mouth dropped open.

"With a diamond that expensive," she said, "and also being in the papers as being stolen, there is no way anyone would be able to sell that. They'd get caught for sure."

"There are black markets," Connie replied. "I'm sure that is how it and other items get sold."

"So, Sean wants to steal something that has already been stolen?" she questioned. "That's totally insane. Does he know where it is?"

"I'm not sure, but he's not going to give up until he finds it. However, it seems that you have distracted him where I could not." Connie smiled. "So, you must tell me everything...how did it happen?"

She was so relieved that Connie wasn't mad at her. She began the girl talk of the first kiss. It felt good to share the experience with someone. Connie was giggling the whole time as they talked.

"That is so much more exciting than my kiss with him," Connie said. "Ours was after a celebration and drinks. The moment was there, and we kissed. But yours is tops."

Jessica didn't tell her about the conversation they had about him feeling the need to protect her from Victor and him. That would be just something she kept between her and Sean.

Jessica and Connie went over the plan multiple times and even acted it out in the living room to make sure they knew what they were doing. When the evening arrived, she helped Connie fix dinner. They made chicken cordon bleu with brown rice and mixed vegetables. It was about 6:00 p.m. when both Bruce and Sean walked in the door.

"Something smells wonderful," Sean said as he came inside. His gaze fell upon Jessica.

"Oh, why thank you," Connie said butting into his gaze. "It's just a little something we threw together. We figured a good home cooked meal was what we all needed tonight."

Sean gave Connie a kiss on the cheek.

"Thank you, and yes, it is," he said. Sean looked again to Jessica. "Did you work on the drop off plan?"

"Yes. We have a good plan, I think." She tried not to look at Sean for too long as her stomach started in on act two of the butterfly ballet.

"Great. Show it to me after dinner."

"Dinner is ready," Connie sang happily.

Sean sat down next to Jessica while Connie sat on the other side. She had a hard time wondering why Sean didn't like Connie. She was a pretty girl. She wasn't afraid of anything, well, except Victor. She felt Sean's leg bump into her leg gently. She tried not to show emotion, but his brief touch sent exciting shivers up her spine.

Right after dinner, Sean pushed his plate away and took the map that Jessica drew and began reviewing the plan. He nodded as he looked it over. She took turns with Connie explaining how it was going to work.

"Good job," Sean acknowledged. "Connie, tomorrow go get the purses and let's make this happen."

"Sweet! I get to go shopping!" Connie giggled.

Jessica stood up and started to gather plates. Sean placed his hand on hers briefly.

"It will work," Sean reassured her. He stood up and gave a wink to her and then headed to his office.

Jessica let out a soft sigh. This was going to be harder than she thought it would be, to just ignore him. All she could think about was kissing him again.

****

Sean brought out of the office a couple of duffle bags. He sat them down on the floor in the living room. Bruce leaned forward and unzipped one of them. They each pulled out a gun and started cleaning it and loading them.

"Why do you have guns?" Jessica asked as she entered the living room.

"For our protection," he said. "Besides, you won't be using one tonight."

"You are still going to make me go, aren't you?"

"Well, I could call Victor to see if he wants to watch you," he thought aloud, "or you could come with us, where it just might be safer."

"I still don't want to go," Jessica pouted a little. "I don't like guns."

"Come here," he told her. Jessica walked slowly closer to him. "Have you ever held a gun?"

Jessica shook her head. From the corner of his eye he could see Bruce grip his gun a little harder. Jessica slowly walked to the side of the loveseat where he was sitting.

"Here." He handed the gun to Jessica.

"I'd rather not," she said quickly.

"It's not going to hurt you," he told her. "Put out your hand."

Jessica stretched her hand out with hesitation. He put the gun gently in her hands.

"It's not going to bite you," Sean said. "It's not loaded."

Jessica relaxed a little as the gun lay in her hands.

"Now hold it like this," Sean said as he moved the gun in her hands and pointed it towards the television.

Jessica's hands were shaking a little as she pointed it towards the television.

"Have you ever had to use one?" Jessica questioned.

"A few times," Sean said as he smiled. "But don't worry, no one got hurt."

"You are giving her a gun?" Connie asked as she finally joined them in the living room after starting the dishwasher.

"No, she doesn't get a gun," he said. "She just wanted to hold one."

"No, I didn't," Jessica said shoving the gun back into his hands.

Sean laughed. Bruce loosened his grip on his gun.

"Sit here," Sean said, "I want to show you how to load one."

Jessica sat in the space next to him on the loveseat. Sean took apart the gun and began showing Jessica how all the pieces fit together then he proceeded to take out the bullets and load them into the magazine while she watched. He slid the magazine into the gun.

"Now, feel how much heavier it is," Sean said as he placed the loaded gun back in her hands. Jessica's hands lowered a bit as she could feel the weight difference. He trusted Jessica as she held the loaded gun. He knew what he was doing. He was gaining her trust and she gaining his. At any moment she could turn the gun on them and try to get out of the house. But he knew she wouldn't do it.

Jessica handed the gun back to him.

"It is heavier," she said. "I'd rather you hold onto it. They make me nervous."

"Just remember, guns don't kill people. People kill people," he told her. "Guns are good for protection, but it is wise to not pick up a gun unless you know how to use one."

Jessica gasped.

"I could have shot you?" she questioned nervously.

"No, Jess, the safety was on." He smiled and patted her leg. "Besides, Bruce wouldn't have let you shoot me."

Jessica flopped back on the loveseat.

"I wasn't going to shoot you," Jessica said letting out a deep breath. "But I could have."

"That's why you aren't getting a gun," Sean kept his hand on her knee and rubbed it a little then went back to loading the other gun.

"Oh," Connie started, "show her what a tracker looks like."

He reached in another bag and pulled out a small device.

"Most likely this will be inside the pouch with the money your mom hands you. You need to take the money out of their pouch, shake it, then put it in the purse that Connie will be picking up for you," he explained. He let Jessica hold the tracker and look at it.

"I hope this works," Jessica whispered.

"Your plan looks great," Sean told her. "Have a little faith."

Connie stood up and looked at her watch.

"I'm going to go upstairs and start looking for clothes for Jessica and me to wear," she told them as she moved towards the stairs.

Bruce grabbed the two duffle bags and started organizing them at the kitchen table. Sean moved his arm to the back of the loveseat and touched Jessica's hair. She jumped.

"What are you doing?" Jessica whispered nervously.

"Touching your soft hair." Sean winked at her.

"Sean, do I really have to go? I promise I won't leave."

"Yes, you have to go because we will be calling your folks afterwards, remember? I don't want to make two trips."

He moved his hand from her hair and touched her cheek. He just couldn't help himself. When she was near, he wanted her to be nearer to him. He thought of kissing her lips all day and he really wanted to do it some more.

Jessica quickly stood up causing his hand to drop to the loveseat.

"I'm going to help Connie," she quickly said and then headed upstairs to the room.

Sean knew he shouldn't be doing this but never in his life had he felt so comfortable with a lady like he felt with Jessica. He really needed to control himself. It was already going to be hard letting her go.

ELEVEN

At 9:00 p.m. everyone gathered around the kitchen table. Everyone was dressed in black. Jessica's heart was still pounding with nervous excitement for all this. She wore a black hoodie with her black jeans. She kept her shaking hands in the pockets of the jacket.

Sean looked at his watch and everyone, but Jessica, looked down at their watches, too. Of course, she didn't have a watch.

"Mark," Sean said as everyone clicked their watch. "Let's go!"

Everyone headed to the back door. Jessica paused. No one blindfolded her. It was as if she was a trained puppy now and she didn't want to go outside without her leash. Sean paused and looked back at her.

"Coming?" He asked.

"My eyes?" Jessica said giving a hint.

"Oh, yeah." He chuckled lightly as he quickly grabbed the blindfold that was sitting on the counter. "I just figured you were a part of the team." He quickly tied it around her eyes and led her out of the house.

"Bruce, you and Connie ride together, I've got Jess," Sean said.

"Ten minutes," Bruce said.

Sean got her in the car and began buckling her up. Jessica heard the garage door open and the other car pull away. Then she felt Sean's lips brush across hers. She jumped. She didn't expect that one.

"You look good in black," he whispered then closed the door.

His deep voice sent chills down her arms. She needed to stop thinking about his kisses and warmth. He was most likely using her, for what, she wasn't quite sure. There is no way he could really like her. Confusing thoughts entered her head again.

He started his car and backed out quickly. He sped down the road and made the turns that she remembered from earlier but also added a few more quick turns confusing her as to where they were going.

"You can take off the blindfold," he said.

Jessica did as she was told. It was dark outside. They passed by the area where they got their breakfast and headed right out of this little town. The city still didn't look familiar to her. She really needed to get out of Winslow more.

"Are we heading towards Winslow?" Jessica asked him. "My directions are messed up."

"No, opposite direction," Sean said. "So, have you thought of what you are going to say to your parents?"

"Not really."

"Remember, you are going to need to act distraught, like you are scared and in danger," he reminded her.

"Kind of like right now?" She asked him.

"Oh, we aren't in any danger...yet."

"How can you do this?" Jessica blurted out. "You do know it is wrong, right?"

"Yes, I know it is wrong," he paused as it seemed like he was thinking of what to say next. "It's like driving a car without a seat belt. We know it is wrong because we could get in an accident and get hurt or possibly die in the crash, but we take the risk. Same here, anything can happen, but I promise you, we do it very cautiously. If anything feels wrong, we abort."

"I feel it is wrong," She pleaded, grasping his arm. "Please abort."

"No, you feel it is wrong because you have never done this before. We aren't aborting, not yet."

Jessica kept her mouth shut. She knew she wasn't going to win the argument. She sat back and looked out the window and watched trees and buildings go by. He turned into a parking lot of a local supermarket. There were still many other cars in the parking lot for being after 9:30 p.m. Sean pulled up next to a couple of cars. There was a gray Trail Blazer parked right next to where Sean stopped.

Jessica saw Connie and Bruce get out of a little sports car and head over to the Trail Blazer. Sean opened the door and motioned for her to get out, too. She did as she was told and hurried around to the Trail Blazer. Sean got in front with Jack and Jessica sat in the middle of the back with Bruce and Connie on the sides of her. It was a little snug.

As they drove away from the parking lot, the group talked about things that Jessica didn't quite understand so she just zoned out and was watching the spots around her. Everybody quieted down when they reached inside another city limits. She missed seeing the sign as to the name of what city they just entered. She really needed to pay more attention. It was around 9:45 p.m. according to the clock on the radio.

"Stick to the plan," Sean told everyone.

Jessica had no clue what he meant because apparently he must say this each time they do something. She did not need to know what the plan was. The less she knew the better.

Sean pulled out of his bag some type of remote computer device or something like that. As they drove slowly down a street that was by a bank she watched him punch some buttons on the remote and then Jack pulled the car around a corner and stopped.

Sean turned back to Jessica and took a hold of her hand.

"Stay with Jack. We won't be long," he said and then he, Bruce and Connie quickly got out and disappeared into the darkness. Jessica's heart rate sped up. Jack drove the vehicle to a darkened area and parked, but with the vehicle running. He turned on a scanner and a walkie-talkie.

"All clear," Jack said on the walkie-talkie.

"Entering," Sean voice was heard over the radio.

Jessica's heart felt like it was in her throat. Her hands were shaking as she tried to hold them still in her lap.

"What did he do with that device?" Jessica asked.

"The less you know the better," Jack told her. "Watch out the side. If you see a police car or security vehicle, let me know."

Jessica quickly looked out the window watching for anything that moved.

"How long does this usually take?" she asked.

"Fifteen to twenty minutes," Jack said. "It's a small bank."

Jessica's heart was beating rapidly, she was looking everywhere she could to make sure she didn't see anything. They sat in silence for what seemed like forever. She glanced at the clock on the radio. Fifteen minutes had passed. Then something caught her eye. It was a flashlight.

"Jack," Jessica gasped. "What is that?"

Jack cussed as he picked up the walkie-talkie. "Company. Plan B."

The flashlight moved more towards the building and Jack put the Trail Blazer in gear, and without lights on started to slowly roll forward. The person who had the flashlight entered the side door. Jack gunned it and sped past the door and away from the building. "They are in." He called on the radio.

"You cannot leave them!" Jessica cried out. "They will get caught."

Jack didn't listen to her. He kept driving.

"Jack, go back!" Jessica's voice was loud. She started pounding on the passenger seat. "They will be caught!" She started to cry. "You cannot leave them!"

Jessica watched as she saw a police car pass them going rather quickly.

"No, no, no!" she cried. "Turn around. We need to stop the police!"

"Jessica, be quiet," Jack said. Jack picked up the walkie-talkie and pressed a different button on it that made a red light flash on their end but nothing else. "Come on, Sean," Jack said quietly. After about a minute, she saw the light flash two times red on their device. Jack whipped the vehicle around and started heading back towards the bank.

Jessica was still sobbing. As they passed the front of the bank there were two cop cars. She started to shake. They were stuck inside the bank and they were going to be caught and go to jail and she'd never see Sean again. Tears continued rolling down her face as she suppressed her cries to not cry out loud. She sucked in her sobs very often.

"When I stop," Jack said to her, "open the two back doors and do it quickly. Move to the middle seat when done."

When they got to the corner of the street Jack stopped.

"Now!" He yelled as he leaned over and opened the passenger side door. Jessica quickly opened the two doors on each side of her and moved to the middle seat as instructed.

In less than ten seconds three people in black jumped in the Blazer and Jack took off. Bruce and Connie were laughing. Sean pulled his black beanie hat off and turned back and looked at Jessica. She still had tears running down her face and trembling.

"Stop at the phone booth over there," Sean said pointing to the grocery store.

"What?" Jack asked. "We need to get away from here."

"Do as I say," Sean demanded.

Jack stopped the car right by the outside phone booth. Sean turned back to Jessica.

"Get out and come with me." Sean opened his door and stepped out of the Blazer.

Connie got out of the vehicle to let her out. Jessica wiped her eyes and followed him to the phone booth.

"You almost got caught," she sobbed. "I was so scared."

"Call your home now," he said.

"What? Why?"

"You are distraught and scared because of the danger...call them now!" Sean picked up the phone and put in some coins.

Jessica dialed her home number. It rang a few times then her father answered the call. Sean was standing right next to her so he could hear what was being said. He mouthed the words "Talk".

"Daddy," Jessica's voice cracked.

"Jessica! Where are you?" her dad asked.

She could hear her mom's voice. "Are you hurt?"

"I'm scared, Daddy," she said. Jessica wasn't lying, she truly was scared. "They let me call you to let you know I'm okay."

"Where are you?" her dad asked again.

"I don't know," she said. "I'm at a phone booth somewhere."

"Ask if they got your letter," Sean whispered.

"Did you get the note?" Jessica asked him.

"Yes," her dad said. "We will get the money, I promise."

Jessica continued to sob. "I just want to come home."

Sean looked at his watch and he motioned for her to say goodbye.

"I have to go. I love you," Jessica said and then quickly hung up the phone. Tears were running down her face. She did miss their voices.

Sean put his arms around her and hugged her tight. Jessica cried on his shoulder. She noticed the lights on the Trail Blazer flicker. Sean took her hand and led her back to the Trail Blazer and was placed in the middle seat again. Jack sped away once Sean was in the vehicle.

"What was that all about?" Connie asked.

"I promised her I'd let her call her family," Sean said. "Proof of life."

Jessica put her face in her hands and leaned forward a bit and continued to quietly cry.

"Why did we have to do it right then?" Jack asked. "We are kind of in a hurry."

"I needed for her to be scared when she called. We've been too nice to her lately and her phone call would not have been convincing. She got scared tonight and so we made the phone call," Sean explained.

"Good idea," Connie said. "You are so smart, Sean."

"Thanks to Jessica, she saw the cop outside with the flashlight," Jack said. "I would have been too late in calling it in."

Sean reached his hand back and touched her hand that was covering her face. He rubbed her hand. Jessica didn't want him to touch her right now. She was extremely mad at him for scaring her.

"Did you get anything?" Jack asked.

"Yup," Bruce said greedily.

****

Back at the shopping center everyone exited Jack's vehicle. Jessica had stopped crying, but she still did not talk or look at anyone. Sean reached in the bag and pulled out a wad of bills and handed it to Jack.

"Later," Sean said as he walked with Jessica back to his car. He opened the door and let her in. Sean hated himself to put her through this. If only Connie, Bruce and Jack didn't pick her up on Saturday. If she was meant to be in his life, he was sure their lives would have crossed at a different time under better circumstances.

"I'm sorry I scared you," Sean finally said. "Sometimes things like this happen."

"You could have gotten caught," Jessica spoke but not looking at him. "Jack wouldn't go back."

"That is part of the plan," Sean told her. "We knew how to get out; we just needed to get out quickly and without Jack getting caught, too. It all worked out. We are okay."

"I'm not," Jessica said sadly. "I've never been so scared in all my life." Luckily her shaking had stopped. "I feel so exhausted now."

"Adrenalin rush and now you are crashing," Sean laughed a little remembering his first time breaking in a bank. "You will feel better, I promise."

"Did the cops even see you?"

"They saw Connie," Sean said. "Just her back side. I'm flattered that you were worried about us. I really thought you'd be rooting for the police to catch us, and then you could go home earlier."

"I'm so confused," Jessica told him. "I'm supposed to hate you all because you have taken me from my family, but you also have been so good to me and have treated me like a friend. I don't know if I'm to turn you in or not. I've grown to like you guys. You are fun to be around, except for tonight."

"I told you we weren't kidnappers," Sean said. "I don't think I'd ever do this again."

"I'm sorry if I messed things up," She told him.

"No, you didn't mess anything up. If they would have left you in the alley, I would have never met you," Sean said. "I'm happy they took you."

He reached his hand over and touched her damp cheek.

"You've grown on me, too," he said, "and I like it."

As they got a bit further down a dark road Sean quickly said, "Blindfold, please."

Jessica pulled the blindfold over her eyes. He dropped his hand to her hand and gave it a squeeze. He turned down the road that led to his secluded home. The car bounced around a bit as he pulled into the garage. Once inside, he turned off his car. Bruce pulled up next to them.

"You can take the blindfold off," Sean said while they were still in the car. "You are safe now."

Jessica helped him carry in the bags and they all gathered around the kitchen table as he emptied the cash on the table. It wasn't a lot, but there were bundles of $20's, $50's and $100's. Connie grabbed some wine that was in the fridge and poured everyone a glass, even one for Jessica.

"Come on," Connie said. "You deserve a sip."

Jessica put the glass to her lips and tasted it. She shuttered and pulled a funny face. The three of them laughed at her. Sean opened the fridge and handed her a Coke instead. Jessica forced a smile. Sean took her glass of wine and poured it into his.

He counted out the money and split it into four portions.

"Not a lot, but not bad for a fifteen-minute job," Sean said as he pushed the money to each of them. He paused and then pushed the fourth portion to Jessica.

"I cannot take that," Jessica shook her head.

"You saved us from getting caught," Sean told her. "You deserve a cut."

"It's not my money," she said. "I cannot take it. I will not take it."

"Very well," Sean said. "Connie will take it and buy you some clothes with it tomorrow morning when she goes and scopes out the mall."

"Yay!" Connie said happily. "Shopping!"

Jessica stood up and put the Coke back in the fridge.

"I'm going to bed," she said. "I'm exhausted."

"Good night," Connie said as she took Jessica's portion of the money eagerly.

"Rest well," Sean said as he winked at her. He watched her go upstairs.

Connie wandered to the living room and plopped down on the couch and turned on the television. She kicked off her shoes and focused on the show as she sipped her wine.

"You know," Bruce said to Sean in a whisper, "you are going to have to let her go."

Sean gave him a quick look then glanced over to Connie to make sure she wasn't listening. He didn't think he was giving any caring type of hints.

"I know what I'm doing," Sean replied taking another sip of the wine.

"She's too kind hearted. She's not your type," Bruce said.

"Stop reminding me," Sean sighed. "She's just so…" he paused, "unattainable?"

Bruce chuckled a little. "That hasn't stopped you before."

"I don't think she will turn us in," Sean whispered low.

"Thanks to you," Bruce said lifting his glass. "If you are only doing this to save our butts, then you'd better not hurt her because she will tell then."

"I like her," Sean whispered. "She's refreshing to be with."

"She is pleasant to look at, too." Bruce smiled then gulped the rest of the wine down from his glass.

"I couldn't bear to hurt her." Sean finished his drink and took the glass to the sink to rinse it out. "She's been making me think, a lot, about what I…we do here. Maybe I should throw in the towel on these heists. I don't want to get caught and spend the rest of my days in prison without her. So, maybe she is my type after all."

"Sean, you are the best thief around. You can't get caught. You know this all too well."

"Still, maybe I need to think about this more." Sean walked down to the couch were Connie was sitting. He put his hands on her shoulders and gave a quick massage. "Play time is over. Head out. More plans still need to be made for Jess's departure. Go home."

Connie turned off the television and moved around to Sean and put her arms around him. Sean held her but not in any type of loving way. He would rather hold Jessica.

Connie leaned in and gave him a kiss. She slipped on her shoes and grabbed her bag of things and both she and Bruce left him alone with his thoughts. He picked up the papers for Jessica's drop off and began reviewing them again. He didn't want her to go.

Once everyone had left he pulled out his phone and sent a text message:

"I'm breaking in tomorrow," he typed. "I'm tired of this game."

"Do you have a location?" a response replied.

"No, but I will find it." He closed his phone and tucked it in his pocket.

TWELVE

Strange dreams filled Jessica's head. She was going into banks and robbing them. Then Jessica was being chased by the police and crying at phone booths. She was being laughed at by Connie, Bruce and Jack. Sean was always right there by her side trying to convince her that it was okay to steal as he dangled the Midnight Star diamond in front of her. Jessica tossed and turned and was having a really hard time shaking these visions from her head. At one point, she remembered crying so hard that she may have actually been crying out loud.

A warm hand touched her cheek. She was lying on her side and she quickly opened her eyes to see Sean sitting on the bed next to her.

"Are you okay?" he inquired. "I heard you crying in your sleep."

"I was crying?" Jessica asked. "Bad dreams." She wiped her face and could feel that around her eyes it was a little damp from tears.

"I was wrong," Sean said. "I should not have brought you with us. I don't know what I was thinking."

"What time is it?" Jessica yawned. Her eyes couldn't focus really well on the alarm clock without her glasses.

"It's 3:15 a.m."

"Why aren't you asleep?" She asked him. "Did my bad dreams wake you up?"

"I couldn't sleep because I am regretting taking you with us. I think my main motive was to indeed scare you so you could make a convincing phone call to your home," he said. "I just didn't realize the heist tonight would cause such a terrible reaction from you."

"It could have gone wrong," Jessica told him. "You all could have been caught. I could have been caught and then I'd have to try to convince the police that I am not a robber and I really was kidnapped."

"But aren't bad people supposed to get caught?" Sean asked.

"You aren't really that bad. You just have a distorted idea of what is right."

"Some things aren't always as they seem," he whispered. "I'm just passing time, I suppose."

"Time for what?"

"Until I can settle down and grow up," he said with a chuckle.

"How long have you been doing this?" she asked him.

"Since I was a teenager. That is why I'm so good at it now."

There was silence between them for a few moments.

"Connie told me that you want the Midnight Star for yourself. Is that true?" Jessica boldly asked as she sat up in bed.

He laughed.

"I guess I'm not as secretive as I thought I was," he said. "Yes, I'm looking for the diamond."

"Didn't you say Victor has it?"

"Yes. He plans on selling it and I need to get to it before he sells it," Sean told her.

"Why do you want it?" Jessica asked again. "You'd go to jail for sure if you were caught with it."

"I've promised someone that I'd get it for them."

"So, are you working for someone else besides Victor?" she wondered aloud. "You don't trust Victor at all?"

"Something like that, and no, I don't trust Victor. He's dangerous and the leader of this gang and he needs to be stopped," Sean reached out and touched her hand. "You are asking too many questions."

"But aren't you just as bad as he is? If you are going to steal it back, then you are a thief just like he is."

"As I said," he stood up. "Things are not always as they seem."

"What are you talking about?"

"Don't worry. I need to get you home." He ran his hand through his hair. "That's probably another reason why I cannot sleep."

"Where are the others? Did they go home?" Her eyes wandered over his bare chest. She could feel the butterflies flipping in her stomach again.

"Yes, they went home shortly after you went to bed. I will let you sleep. I was just worried about you."

"I'm worried about you," Jessica said as she reached out and touched his arm. "Insomnia is not good. I've had that before." She scooted over to the middle of the bed and patted the bed and said, "Come lay. Maybe you will relax."

He hesitated a moment and then he scooted onto the bed with her. They still had some distance between them, but not much.

"Do you want to count sheep or think of counting money?" she jokingly asked.

"No, that never works." He laughed a little. "Sometimes it is hard for me to relax after we do a job, but tonight's was a little different and I think that is why it is weighing on my mind."

"Well, it's over now," she said. "We cannot go back and change it. It is something we both survived and now we have to move on."

Sean scooted down into a lying position with his head on her pillow. She slid down next to him and took her fingers and began rubbing over his eye-brows and between his eyes on the top part of his nose. He closed his eyes. She began to see him starting to relax. She rubbed the temples of his head and then moved her fingers down the side of his face. She traced the outline of his beard and tried not to touch his lips.

"If you don't stop doing that," Sean whispered still keeping his eyes closed. "I may end up doing something that we will regret."

Her fingers stopped in mid motion on his cheek. She gulped. Jessica was pretty sure she knew what he meant. She was not ready for *that*. She didn't know him that well to move to that next step in their relationship. *Their relationship?* What was she thinking? He was exchanging her for money later in the week and she would never see him again. There is no relationship. Why did he have to be the bad guy?

She moved her hand from his cheek and then scooted closer to him and put her head up against his shoulder.

"I'll stop," she whispered. "Close your eyes and rest."

Jessica could hear him breathe deeply. She closed her eyes, snuggling next to his arm and drifted back asleep. She felt peaceful lying next to his warm body. This was so much better than her romance novel.

A faint light shone through the closed window. Jessica opened her eyes slowly as she began to be aware of her surroundings again. She felt a heavy arm draped over her. Her mind was blank from why Sean was in bed with her, but then she remembered that he woke her up and they talked. She carefully tried to move his arm but when she did his arm tightened more around her. She carefully rolled over to face him. His eyes were still closed, he was breathing deeply, still asleep. He was so dang sexy it was hard for her to not want to touch his face and chest again.

Jessica's eyes wandered over his body. He had really good defined muscle tone. His short beard was just the perfect length to not be itchy on her face when he kissed her. His lips looked so soft. His dark hair was messed up, but that was normal for sleeping. He just looked so good.

"Do you know it is hard to sleep when someone is looking at you," Sean whispered still with his eyes closed. She could feel her face grow warm from embarrassment.

"Sorry," she whispered back. "You just look so..." she didn't know if she should say sexy or not. "rested," she finished.

He opened his eyes and looked at her lifting an eyebrow.

"Rested?"

"And..." Jessica started again with a stutter. "Um...well, sexy."

"Now I like that word," he smiled as he pulled her closer to him. "Thank you."

"You are welcome?" she asked. "But, for what?"

"For letting me crash here with you," he said. "I think it helped me actually rest."

"Well, it is your house," Jessica told him. "You could sleep where you want."

"This was nice, to just sleep with you," he smiled and gave her a kiss on the forehead.

"Have you slept with Connie?" Jessica asked bluntly.

Sean looked down at her and smiled.

"In her dreams maybe," he said with a laugh. "No. I've kissed her and that is it."

She hesitated then ran her hand over his chest and she could feel him breathe in quickly. She was playing with fire, she knew. But she just had to do it again, touch his chest because this would probably be the last time she could do it. Sean gave her another kiss, but this time on the lips. It was just a quick kiss and then he sat up.

"I'd better get up," he said, "or we will end up here all day long. I've got too much to do today."

Jessica immediately felt lonely without him as he walked out of her room. Even though she knew it was wrong, she really wanted to hold him some more knowing that their time together was coming to an end.

****

Sean did his best to keep his distance from Jessica in the morning while she tweaked her plan some more. As soon as Connie arrived, he quickly left to attend to some business, business that involved Victor and a certain diamond. Victor lived in a town that was closer to Winslow, so the longer drive there gave him time to think of where to look for the diamond. The last time he was at Victor's he secretly installed a device that tracked when Victor left the house. He had been tracking him during the day to find out exactly where he went and how long he was gone. Today he knew Victor would be at the gym until at least 11:00 a.m. so he had until then, which gave him a good hour to snoop inside the house.

Sean decoded Victor's alarm system and went inside. Nice things that Victor had purchased over the years of his thieving business adorned the walls and corners. Priceless paintings and crystal vases were everywhere. Sean couldn't wait for this guy to get what he deserved. Victor had been hunted by many law authorities and with the right information, Sean planned to lead the cops right to him. But first, he needed to get Jessica far away from this team so he could concentrate on this set up.

Sean looked behind many paintings and under the bed and in closets for a safe. He was coming up empty handed. He knew Victor had it. So, if he was Victor, where would he keep it? Sean glanced around each room surveying everything. Personally, he would probably make sure it was near him for protection or hidden away so well that no one would ever know.

He walked through the master bedroom and kicked up the Persian rug on accident as he paced the floor. Sean walked over the rug to fix the corner and noticed how there was a slight mismatch in the flooring. He bent over and brushed back the rug all the way to uncover a place half hidden under the nightstand and bed.

Scooting lower he knocked his hand against the wood flooring. There was a hollow sound. Sean grinned. He found the hiding place. With his fingers, he followed the opening around to see how far it went. The nightstand and bed were covering a part of this. He took a look at his watch. 10:30 a.m. He had at least thirty minutes to try and move the furniture. Just as he began pushing the nightstand to one side, his phone vibrated in his pocket.

He looked down at the caller id. It was Connie.

"I don't have time for you," he whispered as he shoved the phone back in his pocket. He continued pushing the nightstand. The phone stopped ringing and then it started back up again. It was still Connie. Angrily, he answered the phone.

"What?" he said in a gruff voice. "I'm kind of busy here."

"Sean…it's Jessica…" Connie's voice shook as she spoke.

"What's wrong with Jess?" Sean panicked.

"Victor…he took her." Connie began sobbing.

"Huh? Why? No…that can't be, he should be at the gym."

"Victor showed up shortly after you left. He was checking to see if we had got rid of Jessica yet. When he saw that she was still here, he grabbed her and said he would take care of it. Sean, I tried to stop him."

Sean's heart sped up. He was to protect her and now he failed. No, this cannot happen.

"I'll find her!" Sean said quickly then hung up.

He swiftly moved everything back into place in the room then exited to make sure everything in the house was left exactly how it was when he arrived. He stepped out of the house, recoded the alarm system and hurried to his car and left. Where would Victor take her?

As he drove through the town and the streets, he watched all the oncoming cars to see if he could spot Victor's Rolls Royce. Why would he take Jessica? Only one thought came to his mind and it was not going to be good for Jessica. Jessica's life would be ruined if he took her innocence away.

****

Last night had been terrifying for Jessica but nothing will ever top this one. Jessica was bound and shoved in the trunk of a car that belonged to the man named Victor. Victor surprised Connie and her at Sean's house and became furious. From his conversation with Connie, he was upset because she was still there at the house and to top things off; she had now seen his face.

Victor's stringy red hair and pointed chin were enough to give anyone the creeps. His face was not at all handsome and he looked slimy in all ways. He was taller than Sean, but not by much, and he had large arms. He reminded her of an orangutan.

Her heart hammered from anxiety as she continued to cry while in the trunk. This cannot be happening to her. How could everything turn so suddenly? Did Sean ask Victor to take her and dispose of her because he couldn't? After all, he did leave without saying goodbye this morning.

While in the trunk she tried to stay calm and she paid attention to the turns and she counted in her head how long it took before another turn and so forth. When she was riding with Sean, he purposefully distracted her by talking to her or turning the wheel suddenly to confuse her. She couldn't be distracted this time. She had to pay attention.

After what seemed to be a good fifteen minutes in the trunk, the car stopped. Her heart thudded in her body as she wasn't sure what Victor was going to do to her. Would he beat her? Would he kill her? Would he violate her?

The trunk opened and she struggled for the fresh air. Victor pulled her out of the car and tossed her over his shoulder. He brought her to the door of a small cabin at the edge of the mountain side. He put her down and unlocked the door and dragged her inside.

He sat her down on the couch and then took off the tape from her mouth. She still had tears running down her face, but she didn't cry out, she didn't dare. She remembered Sean telling her one time to not argue with Victor. He brought his hand to her cheek and gently wiped a tear that was rolling down her face.

"Oh, Jessica, you are just too sweet to cry for me," he said. "I believe Sean was holding onto you for himself and well, I just can't have that. You are far too delicate for him. Now me, on the other hand, I just might have need for you."

Jessica shook her head to get his slimy hands off of her.

"W-what are you going to do with me?" Jessica managed to ask.

"Well, first, I need you to look pretty. All these tear streaks have ruined your makeup. I want you to look dazzling as I need to take a few pictures of you."

"Oh, you are just sick." Jessica gasped as she thought of him violating her body. "I'm not going to show you my body."

Victor laughed.

"Oh, even though that sounds like an amazing thing to see, I have something else in mind," he said. He walked over to the bed that was in the corner and he lifted off a sleeveless lavender evening gown. "I need you to put this on. I will let you dress in private. The bathroom there," he pointed to another door, "does not have a window so you cannot escape."

He untied her hands and feet then helped her to her feet. He placed the dress in her hands.

"Go change into this and refresh your face and hair." He demanded.

Jessica hurried into the bathroom and closed the door. She looked around frantically for something she could use as a weapon, but it seemed Victor had taken anything that could hurt someone out of the room. Oh, this cannot be good. *Think, Jessica, think,* she whispered inwardly to herself.

"Don't keep me waiting, Jessica," Victor's voice sounded from behind the door.

As Jessica dressed herself in the beautiful evening gown, she kept praying silently that Sean would come to her rescue. Connie would have called him immediately. But no one knew where they went. She used the dark pink lipstick that was on the counter and coated her lips and brushed her hair to make it look soft.

Jessica opened the door and hesitated before she stepped out. She felt extremely awkward as she had never worn a dress as revealing as this one. The strapless gown fit her body perfectly. It hugged tightly to her hips but gave her enough room to walk without feeling like the dress would rip if she sat down. She pulled her long hair over her shoulders to cover up her insecurity. Victor's eyes gazed over her body as she stepped out. Uncomfortable chills covered her, and she folded her arms to keep herself warm.

"Oh, you are stunning, my love," he said. "Almost picture perfect."

He walked over to the dresser and pulled out a black velvet box. Victor walked behind her and opened the box. She stood facing a full-length mirror that was moved to the center of the room and tried to see what he was doing behind her back. He lifted something in his hands and moved them over her head and around her neck.

"One thing is missing that will make you the most beautiful of all," Victor whispered, "The Midnight Star." The royal blue sparkling diamond encased with white diamonds around it was draped around her neck. She gasped. The necklace was heavy but so beautiful. "How does it feel to have three million dollars around your neck, love?"

The sparkling blue stood out so well against the evening gown she wore. The diamond looked amazing on her. She couldn't help but reach her hand up to touch it.

"You have it," Jessica exclaimed. "The police are looking for this."

"And they will never find it," Victor chuckled. "You are going to be my model. We are going to sell this baby off to get my three million dollars. I just might let them take you as a bonus, too, after I get my cut."

"I'm not going to help you," Jessica blurted out.

"Oh yes you are," Victor brushed his fingers through her hair. He stepped in front of her and positioned the necklace around her neck. "Friday we are going to sell this."

Jessica was to be home on Wednesday. How could she help him on Friday?

"I'm being returned? Sean is going to get ransom for me."

"Not if I keep you here with me." His words left an uneasy feeling in her stomach.

"No, this can't be happening," Jessica tried to hold back tears.

"Oh, no, no...don't cry. I need to take a picture of you." Victor stepped back and pulled out his phone camera. "Now, please smile for me."

Jessica wouldn't. However, Victor took a few pictures anyhow.

"Oh, this is so perfect." Victor grinned. "The diamond looks amazing on you. It's a shame to sell it."

Victor went back to her and removed the diamond from her neck. She was relieved to have that weight lifted from her bosom. He returned the necklace to its box and then put it in a safe that was located behind a picture by the bed.

"You are going to stay with me," he said grinning, showing his coffee and tobacco stained teeth. "I'll just let Sean know he is relieved of his duties with you. Come, let's go back to my place. I have food there; we can have lunch together and get to know each other." He picked up a blindfold and put it around her eyes.

"I need to change," Jessica said nervously backing away from him.

"No, I want you just like this." Victor took his hand and ran it along her collar bone. She stiffened to his touch. He laughed then took her hand and led her outside. The cool mountain air sent shivers over her body. He led her to the car and opened one of the doors and gently pushed her inside. Thank goodness she was not in the trunk.

As he began his descent back towards town Jessica tried to make sure her calculations were correct as to how to get back to this cabin. If she was able to get out of this mess, she would tell the cops exactly where to find Victor and the diamond.

"Won't people think it weird that you are driving a woman who is blindfolded?" Jessica asked with hopes her blindfold would be removed.

"My windows are tinted."

"I'm cold," Jessica said trying to warm her body.

"You complain too much. I think I can see why Sean wanted to get rid of you."

THIRTEEN

Sean had travelled all over the area and couldn't find Victor's car. Frustration flowed in his veins. How could he have been so careless and leave her alone? He decided to make another stop back to Victor's home. As he did, he noticed the black Rolls Royce parked in the driveway. His heart pounded like a drum. If Jessica was in there, how was he going to get her out?

Sean parked far enough away to not be seen. He sat and thought for a moment. Then an idea popped into his head. He made a quick phone call to his superior and explained the situation.

"I have to get her out," Sean told the man on the other end. "She's in danger."

"So, you will get her while he is being distracted by the man at the door."

"Yes. This will work." Sean was determined.

"I'll send him over in ten minutes. But you need to get her to safety today. It cannot wait. We need the diamond now."

"Yes, Sir," Sean said then hung up the phone. He dialed Connie. "I need for you to contact Bruce. We will be returning Jess tonight."

"Is she safe?" Connie asked with a concerned voice.

"I hope so. Call Bruce and have him be ready." Sean hung up the phone and waited.

Waiting was the hardest part. If Victor laid a hand on her, he'd shoot him dead in an instant. He couldn't believe the overwhelming need he had to want to protect Jessica. Just the few hours he had been away from her this morning, he wanted to be back with her, holding her in his arms and kissing her. He could tell that she felt the same way about him by the way she tried not to look at him and then when he did see her looking, she's had a dreamy look on her face. This woman was indeed heaven sent for him, more precious than the diamond.

He'd been putting on an act for so long that he thought he was numb when it came to romance. However, Jessica somehow lit the candle in his heart, and it was now growing larger and engulfed his body whenever she was near. He didn't want to let her go. Life was just so unfair at times. But now she was in danger. Danger for being around Victor and the others and he needed to get her to safety. He would just find her later and hope the flame in her heart didn't burn out.

It seemed like forever before a truck posing as the local gas company pulled up in front of Victor's house. Sean quickly got out and stealthily moved, with gun in his hand, to the back side of the house. He peered through the kitchen window and could see a woman in an evening gown sitting at a table. The doorbell sounded, Victor said something to the woman then stood up and moved to the front door. By the time Victor had turned the alarm off his house to open the door, Sean had the back door security deactivated and the door opened.

Jessica quickly looked towards the back door. Her eyes lit up as she saw him standing there. He motioned for her to come to him quickly. Victor stepped outside the front door as he talked with the guy that was standing there. Jessica stood up and hurried to the back door.

"Sean," she gasped almost in tears.

"Shh, come with me." Sean took her hand and they hurried through the back side of the property and through an opening that led to the house next door. In no time they were in his car and he drove them far away from Victor's house. He picked up his phone and sent a text.

"Oh, Sean," Jessica started to cry. She put her head on his shoulder. "I was praying you'd find me."

"Did he hurt you? Are you okay?" Sean asked quickly.

"No, I'm not hurt," she wiped her tears. "I'm fine now."

"Jess, we are sending you home today. I cannot have you be in danger."

"Victor might come for me," she cried. "I'm scared."

"When you get back, you tell them all about Victor, what he looks like, how tall he is, everything about him. The police will protect you."

Sean drove for about 30 minutes until they reached a motel just outside of Winslow.

"I'm getting us a room," Sean said. "Connie will come with your clothes." He looked her over. "By the way, you look great." he said with a smile. "But why are you dressed like this?"

Her eyes went wide.

"Sean, he has the Midnight Star! I saw it. He put it on me."

"Where is it?" he asked.

"He took me to some cabin. He made me dress in this and he put the necklace around my neck and took a few pictures. He says he's selling it on Friday."

"Where is the diamond?" Sean asked again.

"At the cabin, I think."

"Where is the cabin?"

Jessica shook her head. "I'm not sure. I tried to remember, but I was so scared," she said. "Maybe it will come to me."

Sean turned off his car and took her hands in his and kissed them.

"I'm so relieved that you are alright," he said tenderly.

"Hold me, Sean," she said moving in closer to him, however, the gear shift was in the way.

"Let me get us a room and then I will hold you as long as you want."

Jessica nodded.

"Stay here, I'll be right back." He gave her a quick kiss then got out of the car, tucking his gun back in its holster on his leg. He hurried inside to get them a room.

He kept an eye on Jessica while he filled out the paperwork for the room and they ran his credit card. It didn't take long before he had a key in his hand. He had asked for a room around the back side so he could keep his car hidden from view of the main road. He parked the car and they went into the motel room. It wasn't the Marriot, but it would do.

As soon as he locked the door Jessica flew into his arms. He held her close and kissed her forehead. She looked up at him with wanton eyes. He knew exactly what she wanted, the same thing he wanted. He put his mouth over hers and deepened the kiss with her. She melted in his arms. It was as if he couldn't get enough of her. He brought her back to the bed so they could sit down. That didn't last long. She had laid back and pulled him on top of her and continued kissing him. Her hands went to the buttons on his shirt and she began fumbling to try and unbutton them while she kept her lips on his.

"Jess, honey, stop," Sean said as he pulled away from her. She had managed to get two buttons undone. "I want you so bad, but I cannot do this right now." He touched her face gently. "We need to slow down."

"But you are sending me away." Jessica touched his bare neck that was now exposed. "I'll never see you again."

"I doubt you can keep me away," he said kissing her again, slowly. "I don't know what it is about you, but I cannot stop thinking about you."

Sean's phone rang. He reached for it and looked at the number. He let out a sigh.

"It's Victor," Sean said.

Jessica shook her head. "Don't answer it!" She panicked.

"Shh," he said as he put his finger to her soft puffy lips. He answered his phone.

"Victor, what's up?" Sean asked acting casual.

"Where is she, Sean?" Victor asked sounding a bit crazed.

"Who, Connie?" Sean asked.

"No, the mayor's daughter."

"I left her at my place. Why did you lose her?" Sean raised his voice like he was upset.

"Don't lie to me, Sean. I know she's with you. I need her back."

"Victor, she's not yours or mine to keep. She's not needed in your plans." Sean tried to steer him away from her.

"I need her to model the diamond." Victor said sternly. "She's perfect. Bring her back to me and I'll give you ¼ of the profits."

"I don't have her, Victor. You lost her."

"She couldn't have just gotten away that quickly. You are too good of a liar, Sean."

"Look, I've got ransom money coming in for her. $50,000. We can't back out of it. I'll find the girl and we will turn her in the right way."

"No, I'll find the girl," Victor said as he hung up.

Sean looked at Jessica. She still was lying on the bed. Her hair had fallen off her shoulders exposing her bare neck and shoulders. She looked so sexy. He took his hand and touched her face then ran his fingers over her lips then down her neck. She lifted her neck for him to keep touching her. He forced himself to stop.

Sean's phone rang again causing him frustration. It always seemed when he wished to be close to a woman, his phone would ring to interrupt the mood. He glanced at the caller id. This time it was Connie.

"I've got her," Sean answered. "We are at the Sunside Motel. Room 25. Make sure you aren't followed by Victor."

He then sent another text telling his superior that Jessica was safe, and that Victor confessed to having the diamond.

Jessica sat up on the bed and looped her arm though his. She placed her head on his shoulder.

"So, what if my parents don't have the $50,000 today?" Jessica asked.

"Don't worry, sweetie, they have it," Sean said.

"How can you be so sure? That's a lot of money."

"I just know," Sean replied.

****

Jessica couldn't help but wonder what secrets Sean was keeping from her. She knew he really liked her so that was no secret. But he just seemed like he wasn't telling her the whole truth on a lot of things. Of course, she didn't really know him, she just had an amazing attraction towards him, and she could tell he had that with her, too.

Sean had got off the bed and stood by the window peering out. She felt like Bonnie and Clyde hiding out somewhere. Even though she wanted to continue kissing Sean on the bed, she understood exactly what he had told her. They needed to slow down.

Sean's pacing stirred anxiety in her chest. She sipped on the bottled water that was in the fridge. Moments passed and then he opened the door. Connie slid into the room. She had a bag with her.

"No one followed me," Connie said. She reached in the bag and pulled out a gun and handed it to Sean. "I brought you this, just in case."

"Thanks," he said giving her a kiss on the cheek. "But I had one with me." He patted his ankle.

Jessica's eyes went large. "You had a gun on you this whole time?"

"Yes, my dear," he said. "Didn't you see me with it when I rescued you from Victor? I don't trust Victor at all."

Jessica shook her head. "I wasn't paying attention, I guess."

Connie handed Jessica the bag.

"Here are your clothes." She looked at the beautiful dress Jessica wore. "Can I have that?"

"Yes," Jessica said. "I don't want it. It's too," she motioned towards the top, "revealing."

"Oh, but it fits you well," Sean complimented her. "But, go change, we cannot return you home in that."

Jessica went into the bathroom and quickly changed out of that dress. It was a beautiful dress; it just needed some sleeves or a shawl. Excitement welled up in her stomach. She was excited to go home, back to her family, her home and work; but life would not be the same anymore. Her life would be void without Sean in it. Even though Connie was a thief, she did enjoy the pep talks she had with her. Life would not be the same for sure.

After rubbing off all of the makeup she was wearing, she pulled her hair back and stepped out into the room. Sean and Connie were sitting at the table talking.

"In a way, I guess this will ensure no cops will be around," Connie said.

"I'm sure they will still be there," Sean told her. "So be careful."

"What are we doing?" Jessica asked as she dropped the dress on the bed.

"Connie will take you to the phone booth just before we get into Winslow. You will give your mom a call and tell her that we want the exchange today. Ask if they have the money. If they do, tell them you will call them back giving further instructions," Sean said as he reached over and took her hand and pulled her closer to him. "Then call home when you get to the mall. Tell them to meet you in the food court in fifteen minutes. No cops. Mom comes alone."

Jessica nodded.

"I'll be watching you," Connie said. "We will go in alone. We trust you, Jessica, don't turn us in."

"I won't turn you in. I will tell them that Victor took me." Jessica shivered after saying his name. "I don't like that guy."

"I looked up when the next movie lets out; it will be at 4:30 p.m. When you call your mom at the mall, call at 4:10 p.m. She would arrive at 4:25 p.m., it will give you a few minutes to exchange the money then the theatre will let out and you can begin your 'throwing them off the trail' routine." Sean stroked her hand gently. "Move to that spot that enters the theatre, Bruce will be in there. Quickly leave the purse with the money in it and move on so they don't get suspicious."

"If something doesn't look right, you will abort, right?" Jessica asked nervously. "I don't want you to get caught."

"I will abort if I don't like the way things are going," Sean told her. "Now, I want you to relax for a bit. I am going to leave now."

"No! Where are you going?" Jessica panicked. "What if Victor finds us?"

"He won't," Sean calmly reassured her. "Connie is more prepared now then she was earlier when he took you. She has a gun with her, and she will use it, if necessary."

Sean stood up and did another look outside the window.

Jessica could feel the sadness flowing over her like a waterfall. This was going to be the last time she saw him. There would be no way he could risk seeing her on a normal basis; everyone would wonder where he came from. A lump started to form in her throat. She didn't want to say goodbye.

"Bruce will be at the theatre at 3:45 p.m.," Connie said after looking at her text. She looked up at Jessica and then to Sean. "Alright, I'm going to go use the little girls' room, and, well, give you a few moments to say goodbye." She turned and locked herself inside the bathroom.

Sean faced Jessica. He reached out his hand and motioned for her to come closer. She obeyed. He put his arms around her and held her close. She took in the scent of his cologne so she could remember him forever.

"Will I see you again?" Jessica asked holding back tears.

"Most likely." He kissed her forehead. "I don't think I can stay away from you, but when I do see you, I don't want it to be in secret."

"Thank you for not hurting me." She looked up in his eyes.

"Thank you for trusting me," he leaned down and kissed her tenderly. He didn't kiss her like he did earlier on the bed, but it was still a passionate kiss. "I've got to go. Stick to the plan."

Jessica nodded. Her lip quivered as she tried not to cry in front of him. She had to be brave.

Sean pulled away slowly keeping his eyes locked on her.

She wanted to say 'I love you' but she didn't know him well enough to say those words, even though she felt it in her heart. She smiled at him. He sent her a wink then he left the motel room. No goodbyes; just walked away.

Jessica rushed to the bed and buried her face in the pillow and let out a few sobs. Connie came out of the bathroom.

"First loves are always the hardest to get over," Connie told her.

"Am I brainwashed?" Jessica asked holding the pillow to her body. "He is a thief. I am not supposed to like him."

"Maybe you can change him."

"I probably won't see him again, will I? He just said those words to comfort me. I thought he liked me."

"Well, you do work at a bank," Connie said with a sneaky smile. "Maybe he ought to plan to rob the bank and then you can see him."

"No, that's not right. Maybe he can open an account and add the money to his account often," Jessica said happily. "Then we can see each other all the time."

"Come on." Connie looked at her watch. "Let's go call your home to get this exchange happening."

FOURTEEN

Jessica's insides were a total mess. Excitement filled her since she was going home yet sadness was in her heart for not seeing Sean. Connie stopped at a phone booth outside of town for her to make a very quick call. The call consisted of saying "Plans have changed" to "Do you have the money?" to "Instructions coming very soon." The conversation had to be kept short so the phone trace couldn't take place.

Surprisingly, her father was able to secure the money. Sean was right. He did say her father would be able to get it. She did know that her dad was wealthy, but he was not one to flaunt it. She made up her mind that she would ask her parents to let her move in with them and she would work to pay him the money back. That was the adult thing to do.

"So, are you guys splitting up from Victor now?" Jessica asked as they sat in the mall's parking lot as they waited for the proper time to go inside.

"Considering Sean snagged you away from Victor, I am betting Victor and Sean aren't buddy- buddy anymore." Connie flipped through a magazine. "I am betting Sean is going to be bailing on us soon. I'm sure as soon as he gets his hand on that diamond, he's going to head north."

"What is north?" Jessica asked.

"Not quite sure. New area to conquer, I guess."

"What about you and Bruce? Are you still going to work for Victor?"

"I'm sure you will be giving a good description of Victor, so I think we need to stay clear of him. Maybe we will just go do our own thing."

"Maybe Sean will take you in? You three, well, and Jack, too, would be a good team."

Connie laughed.

"Funny, you are encouraging us to continue to rob banks and jewelry stores," she said.

"Yes, that's not right. But, if you do continue, please don't take hostages."

"Never again!" Connie continued to laugh.

It had been almost two hours since Sean left her side and it felt like a lifetime. Jessica kept watching any car that came into the parking lot to make sure it wasn't a black Rolls Royce. No cars resembled Victor's. It seemed they were safe for now. Connie's watch beeped. Jessica whipped her head towards Connie.

"Showtime," Connie said. "Are you ready?" Connie handed her the two identical small purses.

"No, not really." Jessica held her stomach. "I feel like I wanna barf."

"It will be fine. The ones we need to watch out for are the security cops in the mall." Connie handed Jessica a sun hat. "Put this on as it will hide your face a bit. Don't draw attention to yourself. After you make the phone call go sit in a secluded spot and flip through this magazine." Connie also handed her the magazine she was looking through.

Jessica nodded.

Connie handed her some coins for the pay phone.

"Ok, there is a phone over by the theatre doors. Go make the call. Remember, she has fifteen minutes and to come alone."

Jessica took a deep breath and took the change. She pulled the hat onto her head. Her hair had turned wavy now. Jessica pulled her hair back into a pony-tail and adjusted the hat to hide her face a bit more. She reached for the door to open it. Connie grabbed her arm.

"Good luck," she said. "It was nice to know you. It's been fun hanging out with you."

"Thanks, Connie," Jessica said with a sincere smile. "It's been fun and educational."

Connie slapped her arm. "Go. Good luck with Trent."

"Oh, him," Jessica laughed. "I think I am over him." Jessica opened the door and quickly hurried into the mall.

A few days ago, she would have ran to the first mall cop and begged for help, but today, she was looking around every corner to make sure no one was watching her. Connie had given her a watch earlier. She glanced at the time and found her way to the pay phone. With shaky hands she dialed her parents' number. Her mom answered it.

"Mom, I'm at the mall, in the food court. You have fifteen minutes and you are to come alone." Breathing hard, Jessica hung up the phone.

Jessica scanned the area and found a table in a back corner. She slid into the seat and pulled out her magazine and began flipping through it. Her heart was beating so fast she thought she'd have a heart attack. Time felt like it was moving in slow motion. Every so often she would look up and scan the area. She couldn't see Connie. If she was there, she was blending in perfectly.

The mall wasn't overly busy for a Tuesday late afternoon. But, there was enough people that if she was being followed by cops she could dodge them by blending with the crowds, at least she hoped she could. She wondered if Bruce was inside the theater. What if nothing worked the way it was supposed to? Jessica's hands got clammy as she thought of many different scenarios. She would go to jail for sure for helping Sean and the group. Her stomach churned.

Jessica looked at her watch, it was 4:24 p.m. She scanned the area quickly to see if her mom was there. Finally, she saw her mom come rushing inside the mall. It seemed like she was alone. Her mom held a small purse and she scanned the food court. Jessica stood up and met her mom's gaze. Both of them had tears in their eyes. Jessica hurried towards her mom and as she gave her a hug then her mom handed her the purse.

"Are you alright?" her mom asked wrapping her arms around her.

"Yes," Jessica said. "Now I am." Jessica opened the purse and proceeded to do exactly what Sean told her to do. She shook the money, and nothing fell out. The tracker was most likely stitched into the purse. She pulled out the cash and moved it to one of the purses she was wearing.

"What are you doing?" Her mom asked nervously.

"Swapping the bags. They don't want to be followed."

"Do you know who they are?" her mom asked.

"The leader's name is Victor," Jessica said. "Let me go make the drop and..." she noticed back by the door some men watching them and looking very suspicious. "Did you bring the cops?"

"Of course," her mom whispered.

"That wasn't part of the deal...they may do something terrible." Jessica began looking around the mall more quickly.

"It will be fine. They will catch these guys."

Jessica handed back the empty purse to her mom. It was 4:30 p.m.

"I'll be back." Jessica turned quickly and began walking different paths around the food court as she continued to look for Connie. The plan needed to be aborted. Everywhere she looked now, she could see people that seemed to be watching her. Sean was going to get caught. Everyone was going to be caught. Her heart beat uncontrollably.

People began coming out of the theatre, which thankfully caused more of a distraction as they had planned. Jessica made a turn which was a blind spot for whoever could be watching. This was the spot where she would back around and head into the theatre to give Bruce the money. Just as she was about to make the switch back, someone grabbed her from behind. A hand went over her mouth and she was pulled back into the blind zone.

Jessica's heart beat out of control. Victor had found her, she just knew it. Jessica immediately began to struggle and kick. She had to get away. She heard the man groan as she stomped on his foot.

"Shhh, Jess, stop," a familiar voice whispered in her ear. It was Sean.

He took his hand off her mouth and turned her around.

"Sean! You can't be here! There are cops everywhere."

"I aborted the job. Now, do me a favor," he said. "Act like you don't know me."

"What?" Her eyebrows crinkled in confusion.

Sean pulled her out into the open and headed towards the food court. Jessica's mom and dad were there surrounded by other people that were most likely the police.

"Agent Turpin, good job!" one of the older men in a suit said as they grew closer.

Jessica looked back towards Sean with a completely confused lost look on her face. Sean let go of her arm and gave her a nudge to go to her parents. Jessica quickly ran into their awaiting open arms. She buried her head in her parents' shoulders as they held her tightly.

"Did you see anyone?" a man in a suit asked Sean.

"No, I grabbed Miss Cook as soon as she came into view as instructed," Sean replied. "I think I scared her, though."

"Thank you so much!" Jessica's father said shaking Sean's hand. "You guys will find them, right?"

"Yes, Sir," Sean told him. "We do have a lead and hopefully your daughter can help us with a name of the leader."

Jessica's face was still void of color as she stared in confusion at Sean.

"V-Victor is all I know," Jessica's stutter came back.

"Let's get you to the police station for debriefing," the older man said to Jessica and her parents.

Sean turned and scanned the area with his eyes as if he were looking for someone. Jessica's eyes looked around, too. Where was Connie? Where was Bruce? What was Sean doing?

Jessica and her parents were led swiftly to a limo parked right outside. Once inside, the car sped out of the parking lot with police cars escorting them.

"Are you really alright?" Jessica's mom asked again her touching her face. "Did they hurt you?"

"No, they didn't hurt me. They scared me. Victor scared me." Jessica looked out the back window. She was looking for Sean's car. "Who was that man who grabbed me?" Jessica asked.

"That is Agent Turpin. He's been assisting these past few days in trying to locate you," her father told her.

"Really?" Jessica tried not to burst out laughing. She cleared her throat. "He...he scared me when he grabbed me."

"I'm glad it's over." Jessica's mom put her arm around her daughter.

"He's going to come after me," Jessica said nervously. "Victor told me he needed me. I know he's going to find a way to take me again."

"Let's tell that to the police. Let's see what they can do. Those who took you are still at large and they need to be caught. So, it's not over, but at least you are safe," her dad reassured.

The limo pulled up to the police station. There were already a few reporters lined up. Jessica sunk down in the seat. She did not want to be on television.

"Don't worry," Jessica's father said. "No comment is all we say, and we will let them know a statement will be made later tonight."

Jessica nodded. Their door was opened, and they got out and were immediately rushed upon by the reporters. Jessica's mom kept her arm around her as they pushed their way inside not looking at the cameras. A police-man led them to a conference room where she was offered some water. Jessica pulled the hat off her head and ran her fingers through her hair to poof it back out a bit.

A policeman came in as well as a few men in street clothes. Sean was one of them that came in the room. She sucked in a breath as they closed the door.

"Jessica," the older man addressed her as he sat down in front of her. "We are so happy that you are okay. Did they harm you in any way?"

Jessica looked down at her hands. They were shaking from nerves. She folded them around her body.

"Um-a- the first night when they took me, a-one of them struck my head with something hard. I still have a bump," Jessica said touching the back part of her head gently. "It knocked me out. When I w-woke up, my hands and feet were bound, and tape was over my mouth." Jessica looked up and around the room at everyone. She looked at Sean. He kept a sober look on his face. "I heard Victor come in. That's what the other's called him. I felt so uncomfortable around him." She gulped because now she was entering into a lie. "When he asked who I was and found out that I was the mayor's daughter, he decided to get ransom." Jessica handed the purse that she still was clutching that had the money in it to her father.

"Can you identify them? How many were there?" the policeman asked.

"Besides Victor, there were three others." Jessica took another sip of her water. "I have no idea who they were. They wore masks around me. I've seen Victor, he has red hair, slightly unshaven face and a pointy chin. He was tall and well built."

"Where is their hideout?" the man asked again.

"I don't know, somewhere outside of Windsor. I was locked in a room most of the time. There was a bed in there for me to sleep on. They kept me to myself except today, Victor grabbed me away from the others and was trying to convince me to stay and be with him. Someone from their group got me away from him and helped me get away. I think Victor's team is falling apart. No one trusts him. I'm scared he is going to come back for me."

Jessica did notice that one of the men that Sean was standing next to happened to slightly bump into him, almost like an acknowledgment type of bump. Maybe she was reading too much into this. She needed to talk to Sean to find out what was going on. Why didn't he tell her the truth?

"We will keep you safe, Miss," the man said. "In fact, the man who saved you, Agent Turpin, has been following this group quite extensively. Maybe you will be able to give him vital information that can lead us to Victor."

Sean nodded and smiled at Jessica as their eyes met. She could feel her cheeks growing warm. She looked away quickly.

"I want to go home," Jessica quickly said. "Can I go to your house?" she asked her parents.

"Oh, yes," Jessica's mom said. "We will not leave you alone until this man is found."

"Agent Turpin," Jessica's dad called out. "Will you please come with us back to the home? I'm sure Jessica will assist you with any information you require."

Jessica gulped.

"Of course, Mayor Cook, I will meet you there."

"Thank you for your statement and we will let you go home now." The older man stood up. "We are so happy you are safe."

"Me, too," Jessica said.

****

This wasn't really how Sean wanted this to go. He was supposed to be undercover for this whole job and now his cover was blown, mostly, all because of the careless decision that Connie made in telling Bruce to grab Jessica. He had spent a year preparing to be the thief and convincing everyone in the band of thieves that he was down-right dirty. Luckily, Sean knew what was going to happen at the mall and he had called off Bruce before he even got to the mall. Connie left when he sent her the abort signal from his phone. He didn't approach Jessica until he saw Connie leave.

His cover wasn't completely botched up, but he was going to have to come up with some type of lie or something to ease the concern that Connie and Bruce would be having at this point. He was really tired of the lies. Over the past year they had been easier to tell, but now with Jessica, he didn't want to lie anymore. Right now, his next biggest concern was how he planned on explaining everything to Jessica, in private. He was always nervous inside when he went on the heists, even though the others couldn't see it, but he was more nervous on what he would say to Jessica in hopes that he wouldn't lose her.

Sean followed the mayor's limo back to their house. While following the limo he did call Bruce to let him know that the house was not safe to go to anymore and for them to hang out at their homes. He told him that he would find a place to stay to keep safe and he would contact them tomorrow when things settled down.

Once inside the mansion, they all sat in the living room.

"Miss Cook," Sean began, "please forgive me for startling you earlier at the mall."

"I-a-I'm sure you knew what you were doing. I was just a little on edge. I hope I didn't hurt you when I kicked you," Jessica answered a little coldly.

"I'm good." He smiled at her hoping it would make her feel better. "If you don't mind," he said looking at the Mayor and his wife, "there are some things that I need to discuss with your daughter that are confidential to my case. Is there somewhere we can speak in private?"

"You can take my office," the Mayor said standing up. "Right this way."

Both Jessica and Sean followed the Mayor to the office.

"Thank you, kindly," Sean said. "We won't be long."

They stepped inside and Sean closed the door. He took a deep breath in to calm his nerves. Jessica wandered over to her father's chair and sat down and folded her arms. The action of folding her arms was a clear sign that she was not happy at this moment.

"So, *Agent Turpin*," Jessica began in an accusing voice and emphasizing his name as if it was a swear word, "when did you plan on telling me about yourself?"

Sean walked over to the front of the desk.

"Jess," he began, "I am undercover. I am trying to find the Midnight Star. In a way, I did hint to you about it. Remember, I did say things weren't as they seem."

"But I don't talk in code!" Jessica replied trying to not raise her voice.

"I'm sorry for lying to you, but I had to. When they brought you to the house, everything changed. I had to find a way to get you home safely so I could keep working the case. I'm so close to finding it."

Jessica sat in silence, with her arms still folded.

"Jess." Sean walked around to the side of the desk by her chair. "My feelings haven't changed."

"I don't know if I can trust you," Jessica said looking at him. "Are you a good guy or a bad guy? All the money you've stolen makes you a bad guy."

"Jess," he reached over and took a hold of her hands as he unfolded her arms. "The money is in a safe at the house. I have not spent a dime. In fact, some of the loot I haven't even given to the others. I'm stalling on them. I know it's bad. I have to keep up this image to gain their trust. They are the bad guys."

He brushed his thumbs over her knuckles on her hands until he could feel her softening up to his touch.

"So, you are really a cop?"

Sean let go of her hands and reached into his pants pocket and pulled out his wallet that held his identification.

"I'm not a cop," he said, "I'm a federal agent." He handed the badge over to her to examine. She read over it.

"I was called in right after the diamond was stolen. They needed someone to fit into the group. I know a lot about security systems. A business was created for me to hide under, Turpin Securities. I found my way to Bruce who brought me to the group and to Victor. I gained his trust and I was just about to close in on him when you showed up in the house."

"You sure didn't act like a federal agent," Jessica licked her lips. "Do you flirt with all the ladies you encounter?"

Sean lifted his hand to her cheek and stroked it gently.

"Only the pretty ones," he gave her a wink.

Jessica took his hand in hers and gave it a quick kiss.

"How am I going to act now?" she questioned. "I cannot show that I like you."

"Right now, I need information to find where the diamond is. I need to catch him in the sale."

"Friday, he plans on selling it. He wanted me to model it while he sells it. He had the diamond in the cabin," Jessica said.

"He's probably moved it now." Sean sat on the corner of the desk.

"I might be able to lead you to the cabin," Jessica told him.

"You said you didn't know where it was."

"I was pretty scared there at that moment. As he was driving, I was in the trunk. I was counting out turns and how long it took to get from one place to the other. I might be able to do it again."

"Can you just tell me?"

"No," she said. "I have to be in the car. Not the trunk, but in the car would do."

Sean looked at his watch.

"I cannot take you away from your family, you just got here."

"My clothes are still at my apartment. I need to go get a change of clothes. Will you take me? I feel much safer with you around. If I can help you, I will."

Sean took her hands and stood her up from the chair. He slipped his arms around her waist and pulled her to him. He touched her lips gently with his. It was just a light kiss, but it made him want more, but he couldn't. Her eyes and open mouth was enticing him to give her more.

"I can't," he whispered. "I don't want your lips to get too puffy."

She smiled and kissed him quickly.

"We are going to have to sneak around, I guess," she winked at him.

"I'm such a bad influence on you." He hugged her tight. "You have a press release that you will need to attend for your return. After this, we should go."

Jessica nodded.

"Alright. Let's get this over with so I can be with you," Jessica said.

FIFTEEN

After the press conference, Jessica took Sean with her back to her apartment where she changed clothes and refreshed her face. Sean waited patiently for her in her living room. She kept thinking about all these strange changing events. Sean was the good guy and always had been. Jessica still couldn't understand why he liked her. With Sean's looks he could have any girl he wanted and why did he like her? She was plain and shy.

She braided her hair quickly and stepped out into the living room. Sean was flipping through one of her romance novels.

"Oh, you shouldn't read those," Jessica said as she grabbed the book from his hands feeling embarrassment flow over her body.

"Why? Maybe it can help me be a better lover." His smile warmed her heart.

"Oh, you don't need that." Jessica tucked the book back in her bookshelf by the window.

"You have a nice place here," he said looking around.

"It's lonely. I should have found a roommate," Jessica replied. "So, is that house really yours?"

"No," Sean said. "It's actually a safe house. I convinced Victor and the others that it was indeed mine. It became a good hideout for our team."

"Where do you live? Oh, man, you're not married are you?" Jessica panicked at the last thought.

Sean laughed. He brought her into his arms and nestled his lips against her cheek.

"I would be in so much trouble if I were married," Sean whispered. "No, you are the only one for me."

Chills covered her body as he said that.

"Until this is over with, then you will go, right?" Jessica's eyes saddened.

"I just live in the next town over," Sean kissed her cheek and then her lips. "I'm not going anywhere without you, alright?"

She gulped. He hadn't really confessed his love for her but he sure was hinting around a lot. Jessica slid her arms around the back of his neck and helped herself to another kiss.

"I still don't know why you say those words," Jessica said stepping away.

"I've already told you." Sean followed her to the door. "I find myself constantly thinking about you and longing to be with you. You've done something to me, Jess, and I really like it."

"I didn't do anything." Jessica looked down bashfully.

"You came into my life when I needed you most," Sean said as he pulled her into his arms. She put her head on his chest as she snuggled into him. This was the best place to be, in his arms. He kissed her forehead. "Come on, we don't have time to be distracted right now." Sean took a hold of her hand. "Are you sure you can find your way back to the cabin?"

"There's only one way to find out." Jessica opened the door and they left her apartment. Jessica brought a bag of clothes with her to take back to her parents. As they stopped in front of his car it finally registered that this was not the car they drove the other night. "Where is your car?"

"You just noticed," he laughed as he spoke. "I wondered when you'd say something."

"I've been too stressed, I guess."

"This is a business car, so it has radio, GPS, police lights, and things like that inside it. My car is stashed away somewhere. Besides, we can't go sneaking up on Victor in my sports car, right?"

"True. Should you have back up?" Jessica asked.

"I'll call for it when I think I need it."

"Are you going to blindfold me?"

"Do you want me to?" he smiled teasingly and opened the door for her to get inside.

"It might help," Jessica said buckling up.

They drove out of Winslow and past the motel they stayed at earlier.

"So, you will arrest Connie, Bruce and Jack, too, right?" Jessica asked.

"Yes, they are thieves," Sean said.

"Isn't it going to be hard? You did become friends with them, right?"

"Yes, it will be hard."

"Will you go back to your hideout?"

"Eventually. I do have things there that I need."

"You will need to blindfold me when we get to the hideout," Jessica said. "Victor put me in his trunk, and I counted and tried to memorize every turn. I think if I am in the dark, I might be able to recreate in my mind the turns."

"Very well," he said. "Now you know who I really am, I don't need to blindfold you as we drive. You now will be able to see where you were."

"Did anyone know that you had me?" Jessica asked.

"Yes. I did have to tell my boss. Your parents did not know you were with me. I kept reassuring them, though, when I was 'at work' during the daytime, that you were okay."

"You are too sneaky," she smiled. "You've had everyone fooled."

"So, do you like me better as a bad boy or the good guy?" Sean asked reaching for her hand.

"Both." She brought his hand to her lips and kissed the top of his hand.

After almost forty minutes of driving, she saw the sign entering a city called Smithfield. As they drove through the town, she saw the fast food place they stopped for breakfast.

"Smithfield," Jessica said happily. "That's where this place is."

"Have you ever been here?"

"Oh, earlier this week," she laughed. "No, not really. I don't know anyone this way."

He drove a few turns and then she remembered this particular spot where he had told her to cover her eyes. He didn't tell her to cover them this time. They kept driving through a residential area and then back towards an open field.

Tall trees surrounded a gated area with a big private property sign on it. He slowed down.

"The house is just that way," he told her pointing through the trees. "We aren't going that way, so I'm turning around and I'll let you think about where Victor took you."

He turned the car around and pulled off to the side of the road. He took of his silk tie and unbuttoned the top two buttons on his shirt. Jessica's heart began to race a little as her eyes moved to the spot by his Adam's apple on his throat. She wanted to unbutton a few more of his buttons to trace her fingers over his collar bone.

"This is all I have," he said showing his tie, "to cover your eyes." His eyes then caught her eyes as they were lustfully looking at his throat. "Now stop that," he said smiling as he took the tie and began to blindfold her. "We can do that another time." When the tie was securely around her eyes, he took her hand and then placed it on his bare neck. She sucked in a breath. "Sorry, I couldn't resist." Sean said leaning in and kissing her.

She moved her hand over his neck then she moved it away. She sighed and leaned her head back on the headrest. She needed to concentrate. It was difficult because she just wanted to keep kissing him.

"Okay, when Victor came out of the gate to this road, did he go left or right?" Sean asked.

"Right."

Sean turned right. He watched and listened to Jessica call out directions. A couple of times they had to backtrack. Jessica felt like she was leading him in the wrong directions but after about fifteen minutes Sean slowed down and pulled off to the side of the road.

He reached over and took the blindfold off. Jessica looked around. They were at the base of a mountain. There was a cabin up the hill.

"That's it," she gasped. Her heart pounded with excitement.

"I don't see his car," Sean said. "He's probably back at his place."

Sean drove his car up another path and parked it so it could not be seen from the road.

"Where did he put the diamond?" Sean asked her.

"In a safe," she told him, "by the bed."

Sean reached for the door handle. "You stay here."

"No way!" Jessica grabbed his arm. "I'm not staying here."

"I cannot put you in danger," Sean told her.

"Leaving me here in the car will put me in danger. What if Victor shows up?"

****

Sean knew she was right. Victor could show up at any time. Sean pulled out the gun he had in the glove box. Jessica leaned back in the seat to stay away from it. He checked to make sure it was loaded and ready.

"So now I know why you know so much about guns," Jessica said.

"That's why I wanted to show you how to use one, just in case you need to protect yourself from Victor." Sean opened the door and cautiously stepped out looking around. He listened and couldn't hear anything. The sun was already down so their sneaking around would be easier. Sean opened the door for Jessica and let her out. He held on to her hand. "Now stay close."

Jessica stepped into his arms and pressed her body closer to his.

"Like this?" she teased.

"You are too adorable." Sean kissed her. "But not that close, not yet."

He took her hand and they quietly walked towards the cabin not speaking. When they reached the cabin, he peered into a window. It was empty. He also scanned the room to make sure there was not a security alarm anywhere. He did not see one. He let go of her hand and pulled out a lock picker. Jessica watched him with great interest. He proceeded to unlock the cabin door. She seemed impressed.

Jessica would watch him and then she would also look around to make sure no one was watching them. He gently pushed the door open. Cautiously, he stepped inside and scanned the area again. He tucked his gun in his shoulder holster. All was clear.

"Don't touch anything," Sean said as he pulled her inside and closed the door. "This is the cabin for sure, right?"

Jessica looked around. She nodded her head.

"Yes," she said as she pointed towards the picture above the bed. "He put the diamond in there."

Sean carefully walked to the wall and looked around the picture. He paused as he was just about to touch the picture.

"What is it?" Jessica whispered.

"There is an alarm on the picture." Sean pulled out his little flash light and shone it behind the picture. He then shined the light up the wall and around the corner. He followed the light to the closet in the corner. He opened the closet, shining his flashlight and pointing his gun inside. The closet was empty. He shined the flashlight around until he stopped at a spot inside the closet. "Come here. I need you to hold the flashlight."

Jessica quickly came towards the closet. He stepped inside and then pulled her inside as well. "Shine it right here." Sean said pointing to a box on the wall. She took the flashlight from him and he pulled out that lock picker and began messing with the box. He carefully removed the cover on the box and then looked over the wires. He carefully worked on disabling the alarm. Within a minute, the red light on the box turned off.

He moved back to the picture on the wall above the bed and observed it again. Jessica continued to shine the light on the picture. Sean moved the picture off the wall and a safe was revealed. It was a combination safe. He reached in his jacket pocket and pulled out a stethoscope.

"Keep the light pointed here," he said as he pointed to the lock. "I need you to be really quiet."

Jessica nodded.

Sean began listening to each click as he slowly moved the knob around. Within minutes he was able to get the full combination set. He winked at Jessica and then he proceeded to open the safe. It clicked and he turned the handle and pulled.

Jessica shined the light inside the safe. There was a box inside of it. He reached in and pulled out the box and carefully opened the lid. His heart sunk as all that was in the box was other pieces of expensive jewelry.

"It's not here." He sighed and put the box back in the safe and closed the door. "Let's get out of here." He grabbed her hand and led her back to the car.

"I saw him put it in there," Jessica said as they were safely inside the car.

"He had to have come back for it. If I had that necklace, I wouldn't be keeping it unattended for too long."

"Friday he's going to sell it," Jessica said. "So that means he already has plans."

Sean picked up his phone and dialed in to his superior.

"The necklace was not here, but there were other jewels," Sean said on the phone. "Jessica says he's planning on selling on Friday. You need to be checking the internet for where this will take place."

"We're on it," his boss told him.

Sean hung up the phone feeling disappointed. He really had hopes that the diamond would be there and then this whole thing would be over with.

"I'd better get you back home before your parents call the cops on me," Sean said as they headed back towards Winslow.

"They know I'm safe with you." She smiled as she reached for his hand.

Sean kept thinking as to what else he could do to get this diamond. He needed Victor to trust him. But how? He glanced over at the beautiful Jessica next to him. It would not be good for him to leave her alone. He needed to continue to protect her.

By the time they reached Winslow a thought kept repeating in his head. He kept trying to dismiss it, but it kept coming back. It was a crazy thought and she'd never go for it. He didn't want to do this, but he feared it was the only way. He had to give her to Victor.

SIXTEEN

Jessica walked with Sean, hand in hand, back up to the mansion's door. She was exhausted from today's activities. All she wanted to do was get in her pajamas and curl up next to Sean. However, that would be impossible at her parents' home. Before stepping inside the house, Jessica leaned into Sean so he could encircle her in his arms. He kissed her head and then her lips. She could not imagine anyone kissing better than Sean. It did relieve her to know that he didn't have feelings for Connie. It was just a cover.

"Are you leaving?" Jessica asked him.

"No. Victor is still out there. Knowing him, he has something planned to get you back." Sean kissed her again. "I will not let him hurt you."

"What are we going to do?"

"I have an idea," he said stepping back from her. "I've been struggling with this the whole ride home, but I fear it is the only thing we can do." He brushed his fingers through his hair.

Jessica's heart sunk. She studied his face and he was completely serious and it frightened her.

"I-I think I know what you are going to say," Jessica stammered.

"I need to give you back to Victor," Sean held her in his arms. "Believe me, if there is another way, I will do it."

She placed her head on his chest. She breathed deeply to calm her nerves. She could hear his heart beating which soothed her anxiety. His musky scent would be in her mind all night long.

"He needs to trust you," Jessica said. "By you returning me to him, you are showing your loyalty to him." She looked up into his eyes. "You will protect me, right?"

"With all my heart and strength, I will keep you safe from Victor." He kissed her forehead again. "Your parents are going to kill me," he said chuckling. "Here I just got you back and now I will take you away."

"If they know what is going on, it will be fine. It's my decision, too." She took a hold of his hands. "Let's do this."

They went inside the house and found her parents in the study.

"We were getting worried about you," Mrs. Cook said as they came in.

"You have nothing to worry about," Jessica said. "I'm with Sean."

Her mom gave her this strange look like she knew she was hiding something.

"Sir," Sean began. "I need to tell you both something."

"Come sit," Jessica's dad said motioning to the couch.

"Agent Kramer mentioned earlier that I had been highly involved in this case with those thieves. They are the ones who took that diamond last year. I've been doing undercover work to-" he paused as if he was unsure what to say. Jessica held her breath as Sean finished his sentence. "Become close to this team and earn their trust."

"You know them?" The mayor asked surprised. "Then why didn't you arrest them?"

"I don't have the diamond. Once I have the diamond, I can arrest them."

Jessica's mom looked concerned.

"If you worked closely with them, then did you know they had Jessica?" Mrs. Cook asked.

"Mom," Jessica quickly said. "Sean was the one who got me out safely." She didn't want her parents to know how involved he was in this group. They didn't need to know.

"I'm sorry I couldn't tell you sooner," Sean told them. "I couldn't blow my cover."

"Then why are you saying this now?" Jessica's dad asked.

"Because Jessica said the diamond is going to be sold on Friday. Victor wants her back. He thinks I'm still a thief. I need to gain his faith in me again. I need to take her to Victor."

"What! No!" The mayor's voice grew loud.

"Dad, it's the only way," Jessica replied. "Besides, Sean will be protecting me."

"How?" The mayor asked.

"I will not leave her alone. I cannot tell you the plans, only that she will be safe, I promise," Sean reassured. "However, to make this legit, I'm going to have to kidnap her...again."

Her dad stood up and paced the floor. Jessica stood up quickly and went over to her father and placed her hand on his shoulder.

"It will be okay, Dad," Jessica said. "I trust Sean. You can trust him, too."

"I will guard her with my life," Sean told the Mayor. "But when I do this kidnapping...you need to be shocked...just like you were the first time. You need to immediately call police and media. Can you do that?"

"If this is the only way," Jessica's dad said. "Then yes."

"Right now, this is the only plan I have," Sean stood up and walked towards the mayor and stood next to Jessica. "Your daughter means a lot to me, I won't let Victor harm her."

Jessica smiled at his loving words. She wished he would show her more how much she meant to him.

"How can she mean so much to you when you don't know her?" her dad asked.

"I've had time to get to know her over the past few days," Sean replied. "She is an amazing and brave woman. I promise to keep her safe."

"Nothing better happen to her," the mayor said putting his arms around Jessica. "Do I have your word?"

"You have my word," Sean said solemnly.

Jessica walked with Sean and her father to her bedroom on the second floor. Sean went inside and moved to the window and looked out. He shook his head.

"I will stage a break in at the kitchen, I think it will be easier there," Sean finally spoke. "You can tell the police that she went for a nighttime snack, peanut butter sandwich or something." His eyes wandered to Jessica. She could feel her cheeks growing warm as she remembered their moment together. She quickly looked away.

"Very well," her father said. "What time?"

Sean looked at his watch. It already was nearing 10 p.m.

"2:00 a.m.," he said.

"I'll be ready," Jessica replied.

****

Sean contacted Agent Kramer and explained his plan to him. The team had found the bidding internet site for multiple pieces of jewelry. It did not exactly say The Midnight Star, but it gave a very good description of the deep blue diamond. Sean took a powernap to refresh his tired eyes. Jessica and her parents had retired to bed. His watch beeped at 1:30 a.m. to get him up.

He tossed water on his face and went into the kitchen. He pulled out some rubber gloves that he kept in his jacket pocket and put them on. He pulled out the peanut butter, bread and jelly. He even went as far to spread the peanut butter on the bread. If there was another way to get the diamond, he'd rather do it, but he couldn't think of another way.

Sean quietly went upstairs to Jessica's room. He opened the door gently and stepped inside. Jessica was asleep in her bed. She was dressed in a cute yellow pajama pant set. He would rather just curl up next to her and fall back to sleep, but business needed to be done first. He softly shook her to wake her up. She smiled dreamily at him as she rolled over.

"Come on, sweetheart," he whispered. "It's show time."

She sat up and blinked her eyes then patted down her hair. She yawned then stepped out of bed and put on her slippers. Sadness filled her eyes.

"I wish I could change clothes," she said.

"But then it won't look right." Sean took her hand and led her out of the room and down the stairs to the kitchen.

She smiled when she saw the peanut butter out on the table.

"Did you plan on doing that to me the other night?" she asked.

"No," Sean admitted. "You just looked so hot in that nightgown and I couldn't resist."

She stepped to the counter and stuck her finger in the peanut butter and brought it up to his lips. He partook of the offering she provided him. She sighed again as tingles filled her stomach. It was just as exciting as him doing that to her the other day. She couldn't believe how bold and spontaneous she had been lately with Sean. This was so unlike her. She felt like she was a character in one of her romance novels.

"Stop," he said as he quickly kissed her. "You are teasing me again. It's a crime to be passionate with you right now. We have work to do."

Sean stepped over to the window in the back door. He reached in his jacket pocket and pulled out his black beanie hat.

"Ready?" he asked.

"No, but I can't wait any longer."

While still wearing his gloves, he opened up the back door and took the lock pick from his jacket and messed around with the lock and then he broke off the lock. He reached for her hand and she took it. As they stepped outside the cool air brushed across them. They left the back door open and knocked over a couple of planters on the way out to make it look like a struggle. Sean led her to his car quickly.

Sean turned on the heater so Jessica wouldn't get cold. She scooted a bit closer to him, the best she could. He drove them to an apartment building that was closer to the police station. They drove into the parking garage. He parked the car next to his silver Camaro.

"So, here is where you stashed it," she smiled. "Do you live here?"

"No, I usually am at the house in Smithfield. But I stash my car here when I am in agent mode."

They switched vehicles.

"I need to call Victor," he said. "And, I'm going to also have to tie you up when I deliver you to him."

"I understand," she said. "Just don't knock me out. I think my bump has finally started to go away." She touched the back of her head.

"I won't do that. Do you think you can put on a good act while I make this call, like you are screaming or something with tape over your mouth? So put your hand over your mouth and make noise." Sean instructed. She nodded. He pulled out his flip phone and dialed Victor.

The phone rang a few times then the tired voice of Victor answered.

"This better be good, Sean," Victor grumbled. Sean could tell he woke him up.

Sean nodded at Jessica to start making noise.

"I got her," Sean said.

"What?" Victor's voice sounded more alert.

"I knocked out the guard that was watching the mayor's house and grabbed her as she was making a nighttime snack."

"You are lying." Victor said. "I know you care for her. She's beautiful, how can you not care?"

"Listen," Sean moved the phone so it would pick up the whimpering from Jessica. "I don't care for her, Victor. I was actually hoping to make her my stress relief, but she is quite stubborn." Sean moved his hand to her face and caressed it gently. "The others don't know I have her again. This is just between you and me."

"So, we should break her, huh?" Victor laughed.

"No, we use her. With her beauty she will be able to sell that necklace with a high price. After the sale, we can get rid of her."

"I say we sell her too," Victor suggested. "Many will buy a beauty like her."

"As you wish," Sean agreed. "When do you want her?"

"Bring her by in the morning. I'll have a room made up for her."

"One thing, Victor, she's part mine, too. I'm not letting her out of my sight."

"You don't trust me?" Victor laughed.

"You don't trust me either," Sean snarled back. "8:00 a.m. I'll bring her by then." Sean hung up the phone.

Jessica let out a sigh.

"Don't let them sell me, Sean," Jessica said nervously. Her eyes were sad.

"Never." Sean started the car and drove it out of the parking lot.

"Where are we going now?"

"Back to my place, of course, we need some sleep. " Sean reached over and took her hand in his. "I promise, nothing will happen to you."

They drove in silence for the next 45 minutes. Jessica had laid her head back on the seat and closed her eyes to rest. Sean had to be crazy to be giving her to Victor. Out of all the stupid things he'd done while undercover, this one was tops. He could not have any harm come to Jessica. She was becoming someone important to him.

He glanced over at her in the darkness and her facial features came into view as they passed by each highway light. Her eyes were closed, and she looked like she was asleep. Her wavy long hair was resting on her shoulder. From the moment he spoke to her alone on that first night, she hadn't left his mind. Never had one woman turned him into a man who melted when he saw her smile.

He pulled up to the safe-house in Smithfield and did a quick glance around the property to make sure everything was secure then they went inside the home. He reset the code for the house to a different password then secured the home. Jessica stood looking around the house. The lights were off, except for the one leading up the stairs. Sean took her hand and led her up the stairs. He paused at her room that she had occupied earlier in the week.

"Go get some sleep. We will be leaving at 7:30 a.m.," Sean told her.

"I hope I can sleep," she replied. She stepped closer to him and he put his arms around her.

"Try your best," he said kissing the top of her head. "We have three more days of this. He's going down Friday for sure."

Jessica pulled away slowly.

"You sleep, too," Jessica said giving his hands a squeeze. She backed away into the bedroom and climbed upon the bed.

Sean turned to leave and then he said what he had always said,

"If you need anything, I'm just in the next room."

He didn't wait for her to answer; he just headed to his room. It was just after 3 a.m. An energy drink would be needed tomorrow for sure. He removed his shirt and shoes and hung his slacks in the closet and pulled on his sleep pants. He stepped into his bathroom and looked at the dark circles starting to form under his eyes. So much was going through his mind there would be no way he could sleep. This job needed to be done quickly. Lack of sleep was starting to make him feel like a bitter person. He didn't understand how Jessica could like him. This job had made him into someone he never was, a liar and a thief. Sean wished he wouldn't have taken this assignment. Maybe his work was testing him. He'd better get a good raise when this was over with.

Turning off the bathroom light, he stepped back into his room and walked to his bed. He stopped quickly as he looked at the beautiful angel snuggled under the blanket on his bed. A grin crossed his face as he gazed at Jessica.

"What are you doing?" Sean asked.

"You said if I needed anything…" Her smile melted his heart.

"What do you need, my dear?" He slid into the bed next to her.

"You." She put her head against his shoulder.

"Now I won't sleep for sure," he said as he kissed her lips gently.

"Just let me sleep by you," she said placing her warm hand on his chest.

"Sleep, Jess. Just sleep." He kissed her again and pulled her into his arms and snuggled with her until they both fell asleep.

SEVENTEEN

Duct tape covered Jessica's mouth and hands while a blindfold was draped over her eyes. She was lying down, scrunched up, in the small back seat of his Camaro. He told her to put up a struggle and act it out really good when he brought her into Victor's home. That's what she agreed to do. Sean pulled up into Victor's driveway and texted him to open the garage door. The garage door went up and Sean pulled his car inside.

He pulled down the front seat and pulled her out of the car gently.

"Show time," Sean said as he gave her hand a squeeze.

He picked her up and draped her over his shoulder and she began kicking and trying to scream as he carried her into Victor's house.

"What did you bring me?" Victor asked laughing as he sipped his coffee. "A badger?"

"She's been at this all night," Sean said as he placed her on a chair in the kitchen and began tying her up with the rope that was by the chair that Victor left for him. Jessica kept wiggling and making it hard for him to wrap her up tightly.

"We should sedate her," Victor suggested. "I don't need to hear her all day long. We have things to discuss."

"Suit yourself," Sean replied.

Victor went to a cupboard and pulled out some pills. He looked at the name and then tossed the bottle to Sean.

"Make her take this," he said.

Sean looked at the label. It was just a moderate sedative, Lorazepam, thankfully, it wouldn't harm her. The dosage was a little higher so she would feel the effects quickly. Hopefully, it would just make her drowsy and she could sleep it off. Maybe that would be best for her right now anyway. He took out bottled water from the fridge and one of the pills.

"Jess, sweetie," Sean said touching her face and talking softly. "Trust me, this won't hurt you."

He carefully pulled the tape from her mouth and she let out a big scream. He covered her mouth again with the tape while Victor laughed. Sean joined him in the laugh, even though he didn't find it amusing.

"Jess," Sean said taking a hold of the back of her hair and pulled on it slightly with force causing her head to tilt back. "Don't make me hurt you. If you scream, I will hurt you."

Jessica whimpered a bit. He knew he wasn't pulling hard on her head and he really hoped she knew he wasn't going to hurt her. He pulled the tape from her mouth again.

"I HATE YOU!" Jessica screamed.

"Ah, a civil word," Victor laughed. "Stand in line, sweetheart, I'm sure there are others who hate Sean, too."

Jessica's head turned towards Victor's voice. With the blindfold still over her eyes she couldn't see him.

"I hate you, too!" Jessica's words were directed for Victor, too.

Sean pushed a pill into Jessica's mouth and put the water to her lips.

"Drink." He said as he poured the water into her mouth. She let the water drip down her face. He kept her mouth closed. "It will just make you sleepy."

Jessica started to whimper again, and tears started falling from under the blindfold. It broke his heart. He waited until she swallowed before he moved his hand away from her mouth.

"Good girl," Victor said. "Take her to the basement." He continued sipping his coffee. "I want to eat my breakfast in silence."

Sean untied her then stood her up and pulled her with him to the basement door. He picked her up over his shoulder again and descended the stairs carefully. There was a couch downstairs and a wooden chair. He placed her on the wooden chair and began restraining her again.

"It was a sedative," Sean whispered in her ear as he tied her up. "It won't hurt you. It might make you feel slightly disconnected with everything and it will most likely make you drowsy. Take a nap; it will help things go by quicker for you. You are okay, Jess, I promise."

Jessica nodded her head.

He took a quick look behind him to make sure Victor wasn't watching them. He ripped off another strip of duct tape and then he quickly kissed her lips. She hitched a breath as his lips met hers. He placed the strip of duct tape over her mouth, again, as he touched her cheek tenderly.

"I'll be back," he whispered then he walked back upstairs.

Upstairs, Victor was waiting for him.

"Who helped her escape?" Victor's voice was stern.

"Bruce," Sean said. "Connie called him. They took her directly to the mall and started the plan to get the ransom. They turned on me. We were to do this together."

"Did they get the money?" Victor asked.

"No. When I caught wind of what Bruce and Connie were up to, I headed to the mall and saw the place was swarming with cops. I sent them both a note to abort job ASAP. I should have let them stay there and get caught."

Victor was silent. Sean was hoping he believed the lies.

"We have a job tonight," Victor said. "Ten o'clock we leave."

"I cannot trust Connie and Bruce," Sean said. "You are going to have to come with me to do it."

Sean's plan was to keep Victor occupied so he wouldn't bother Jessica. That was the only way he knew to keep her safe at this point.

"What about the girl?"

"That sedative will keep her knocked out off and on most the day. She will be groggy when she wakes up. You've got a good lock on the basement door. She's not going anywhere."

"Well, I don't have time to babysit her all day," Victor snarled. "I need to get things set up for the sale."

"50/50," Sean said quickly.

"No, 20/80. You didn't steal the Star, I did. You only got the girl."

"30/70. She's a handful and she will add more money to the sale because of her beauty."

"Fine." Victor huffed. "You watch the girl and attend to her needs. Don't be nice to her like you were earlier this week."

"I did that so she wouldn't turn us in," Sean said. "And guess what, she didn't say our names!" He grinned. "So, it worked." Of course, he didn't say that she told them it was Victor.

"Get in touch with Jack," Victor said. "We need him to drive tonight. Also, tell Connie I want that dress back."

"Done." Sean pulled out his phone and started to dial Connie first. Victor walked away.

"Sean," Connie's voice frantically answered on the phone.

"I need the dress back. Drop it off at Victor's," Sean ordered. He knew Victor could still hear him.

"What are you doing?" Connie asked. "We let her go."

"Haven't you seen the news?" Sean asked.

"Did Victor take her?"

"No, I did." Sean didn't want to go into detail. "We need the dress back now."

"Sean, you are confusing me," Connie's voice was worried. "I thought you liked her."

"Just do as I say."

Connie gasped. "You are going to set him up, aren't you?"

"Now, Connie. Goodbye." Sean hung up the phone. The less she knew the better.

Even though the group all needed to be arrested, a part of him hoped that Bruce, Jack and Connie would make a run for it. Yes, he had grown closer to them as friends and really hated to see what was coming for them, but the bad guys needed to be punished, as Jessica would say.

Sean made arrangements with Jack then about lunchtime he wandered downstairs with a sandwich to give Jessica. Her head was hung down. He took off her blindfold and then the tape over her mouth. She opened her eyes wearily; they had a faraway look in them. She gave him a forced smile.

"Sorry, sweetie," he whispered. "It really is for the better right now. It keeps you safe."

A tear leaked from her eye. He ran his hand over her head and held the sandwich for her to take a bite. She did. She didn't say anything to him.

Every hour Sean would go downstairs and check on Jessica. He put a blanket over her to make her feel safe. At one point he even untied her from the chair and let her lay on the couch and sleep. Connie had brought the dress over to him and he hung it up in the closet downstairs.

All afternoon, Victor was setting up personal invites from his circle of friends for the sale. Sean received a text from his superior telling him that there was notification on the dark website of a date change for the sale. It was going to happen on Thursday, not Friday. Victor didn't say anything to him about that. He guessed Victor didn't trust him either.

****

Jessica wasn't sure if it was night or day. That sedative pill really messed with her mind. She remembers, in a hazy state, Sean coming in and checking on her, feeding her, letting her go to the bathroom and whispering words of encouragement. The drug had finally moved mostly out of her system and now she felt depressed.

The house was very quiet right now. She was tied again to the chair, but her blindfold was off and there was a light on in the room. She struggled to get out of the ropes. Today was terrible. Now she was extremely happy that when Bruce and Connie took her on Saturday that they treated her nicely. This treatment of being drugged and tied up all day was not good at all.

Her mind, when it started to clear, kept her guessing about Sean. She knew he was an FBI Agent, but could this past year have turned him more into a criminal? Could he really want the diamond for himself? When Sean first put her down here and locked the door upstairs, she did hear him telling Victor that he did what he did to get her to not tell the cops. It did make her second guess his actions towards her. He was just using her, she knew it.

She saw the strapless lavender evening gown hanging in the open closet downstairs. Some sparkly white pumps were on the floor next to the hanging dress. She was going to have to go through with this after all.

Jessica wished that her life hadn't become so stressful in one week. She was hoping for her quiet life, once again working at the bank. Would Trent notice her now? Did she want Trent noticing her? Her mind quickly wandered back to Sean. He was so perfect for her, but was it all an act?

From upstairs she heard a door open then close loudly. Heavy feet stomped across the floor along with arguing voices of Sean and Victor.

"You need to trust me." She heard Sean say. "You almost got us caught."

"Look, it's not my fault the team bailed on you," Victor said. "That's why I leave this type of stuff to you guys."

"It was no different than stealing the diamond," Sean told him. "Follow the plan...that's what we do."

"Well after the sale I shall have enough to jump this country and no one will care about these silly banks again."

"Speaking of which," Sean continued, "my internet sources tells me you've changed the date."

"Your internet sources?" Victor questioned.

"It's no secret, Victor, you know I want that diamond and if I have to bid for it like everyone else, I will."

"You don't have that type of money," Victor said laughing.

"I'll steal the money. You know I can do it. I'm the best you've got."

"I'm not sure about that," Victor said. "Justin was quite good."

"You got Justin killed because you changed the plan at the last minute, almost like tonight."

Silence filled the upstairs. Jessica listened. She had no idea who Justin was that Sean spoke of.

"Don't you dare talk about Justin's death, it was all an accident." Victor finally spoke. "I don't want to discuss that anyway, we need someone here tomorrow to dress our doll up," Victor continued, changing subjects. "I've got tickets this weekend to get out of the country."

"Shall I call Connie in?"

"Yes," Victor agreed, "even if you have to bring her here at gunpoint."

Footsteps went over the floor as Jessica looked up at the ceiling trying to figure out what they were doing.

"Go check on our guest," she heard Victor say. "Then camp out downstairs to make sure she doesn't leave. I'm sure the drug has worn off of her. Keep her quiet. I don't want to be disturbed while I try to sleep."

She heard the upstairs door unlock and someone step inside the stairwell then the door closed. Sean entered the room. She tried to smile but the duct tape prohibited that. He walked over and rubbed his hand over her hair and cheek.

"Doing okay?" he asked softly.

She nodded.

He pulled the tape from her mouth so she could have a drink.

"What's going on?" she whispered.

"It's happening tomorrow," Sean replied. "Connie will come and dress you and make you up."

He untied her and helped her to her feet.

"Walk around to get some blood flow moving through your legs," he said as he kept a hold of her arms and walked with her.

"Am I on the news again?" she whispered.

"Yes, everyone is out looking for you."

"Who is Justin?"

Sean took another glance up the stairs then whispered back to her,

"When the diamond was stolen, a man was shot during the heist. His name was Justin. He knew ways to break into high security places, kind of like me. Something went wrong, Victor changed the plan, and Justin was killed by a guard from the armored truck and Victor got away."

"I heard you say he didn't follow the plan. Don't die on me, Sean," Jessica said stopping. She looked up at him. "You are going to call for backup, right?"

"Soon. It's after midnight," Sean told her. "We need to sleep. I want you to take the couch here and I'm going to be on the recliner over here. This will be over with soon."

"I want to go home," Jessica whined a little. "I don't like it here."

"I want to go home, too." Sean leaned over and gave her a quick kiss on the cheek. "I'm so sorry to have to put you through this."

"I agreed to it, remember?" she put her head against his chest and snuggled in closer.

Jessica curled up on the couch with the blanket over her and closed her eyes again. For now, she was just going to have to trust Sean and hope he knew what he was doing and that he was not the bad guy.

EIGHTEEN

Jessica's brown hair hung long over her shoulders and the top was styled perfectly. Connie stood beside her, adding fake long eyelashes to Jessica. It surprised her how well the eyelashes made her eyes stand out. The lavender strapless dress hugged her slender figure nicely. Connie moved Jessica's glasses out of the way and set them aside.

"Once again," Connie said boastfully, "I did a spectacular job."

Jessica smiled and nodded.

Jessica nudged Connie's arm. "You really should change your lifestyle and become a beautician."

Connie sighed and nodded.

"I tell you, that Trent guy is really missing out on you. I feel this whole week has completely changed you. You are a more confident person, wouldn't you say?"

Jessica shrugged her shoulders. "His loss, I suppose."

Connie picked up her bag and smiled.

"I hope all goes well," she said as she exited the room.

Jessica gazed at herself in the mirror. She definitely wasn't the same looking woman as earlier this week. She was indeed beautiful.

****

Sean passed Connie as she was leaving the room. He set his briefcase down on the floor and closed the space between him and Jessica, taking her cold hands in his.

"Jess, you are gorgeous."

She wasn't just pretty; she literally took his breath away. He felt underdressed standing next to her. His black suit coat over a white shirt, and his black slacks just didn't seem to be enough. Sure, he had the looks of an FBI Agent, but he felt as if he should be dressed as a GQ model since he'd be with Jessica.

He stepped back, breaking their contact. He reached inside the leather briefcase and pulled out a gun and a leg holster.

Jessica gasped. He moved in front of her again, gazing into her wide eyes. Her breathing had suddenly quickened.

"Do you trust me," he whispered low. "I need to know."

"Y-yes, I think so."

Sean bent to one knee in front of her and grasped the hem of her dress, lifting it up. She hitched a breath and slapped his hand.

"Excuse me, what are you doing?"

"Trust me," he said. His hands slowly moved up her leg, caressing her leg as his hands travelled upward. When he reached her thigh, he looked up at her face and her eyes were closed. He could see she was enjoying his touch as much as he was enjoying touching her. His heart raced as he caressed her thigh. Her breathing was quick as his hands encircled her left thigh as he wrapped the gun holster around her and strapped in the gun. He tightened it. "How does that feel?" He spoke in a low seductive voice. He paused with his hands on her leg as he gazed up to her face.

"Your hands on my leg or the gun?" Jessica asked with a twinkle in her eye.

His face grew warm and he was sure she could see his face brightening with color. Her smile widened, seeming more victorious.

"The gun silly," He said dropping his hands from her leg and standing up.

"Awkward," she giggled. "However, I succeeded in making you blush."

"Indeed, you did."

He straightened her dress and stood back.

"You look good." He flashed a soothing smile and her shoulders relaxed.

"Why did you give me the gun strap?"

"Safety first," he winked.

"I cannot use a gun," Jessica warned him.

"And you won't." Sean took a hold of her hand and gave it a romantic kiss. "Come on. Let's get this over with."

Victor drove the three of them to a warehouse in the next town. He was dressed in a suit like Sean was. Sean sat in the back with Jessica and she fidgeted the whole time. When they pulled up to the warehouse the sun was setting. Jessica put her arm through Sean's as they walked behind Victor up to the doors of the warehouse.

The door opened and a big burley man in a suit opened the door. He let them inside. Sean's eyes wandered around the inside of the warehouse. The room was dark with a few spotlights in different corners. There were computers and cameras set up all over the room. This was where Jessica would stand as they live streamed the footage of her and the diamond necklace. Sean counted at least ten other men around the room. This was more than he had expected.

Sean emptied his keys and anything metal on a table, just like if he was going through airport security. Another man began patting Sean down checking for any guns. The man patted Sean on the back and motioned for him to step inside the warehouse. Sean picked up his keys and phone and tucked them back in his pocket. Victor was patted down as well.

"Wait," one guy said as he pointed to Victor's big belt buckle.

Sean looked to where the man pointed. Victor's gold and silver belt buckle had the shape of a small snub nose pistol set into the belt buckle.

"That needs to come off," the man said again.

"Wow, Jackson, relax, man," the other man said, "Victor is a regular. He's clean. That's just his bling, it's not a real gun." He motioned for Victor to come through.

Victor clutched his laptop as he joined Sean.

"What about her?" Jackson pointed to Jessica.

"She's the merchandise," Victor instructed as he pulled her to them. "No one touches the merchandise."

Sean put Jessica's arm through his and they followed Victor to the nearest wall of the warehouse. The man, who walked with Victor, opened a door for them and motioned for them to enter. Victor put his laptop down on the metal table and plugged it in. Sean could feel Jessica trembling as she stood next to him. He patted her hand to calm her down.

Sean continued to look outside the room at each person there. He was definitely going to need backup. Victor pulled from his suit coat pocket a large box. He opened it up and revealed the prize diamond that Sean had been searching for: The Midnight Star.

"Your beauty is not complete without this," Victor said as he attached the heavy diamond around Jessica's neck.

The blue diamond sparkled when any light shone on it. It looked stunning around Jessica's neck. For a moment he forgot what he was assigned to do.

"Not only am I going to get money for this diamond; I will get a hefty price for you, too, Miss Cook." Victor ran his hands down her arms. She shuddered.

"You can't do this," Jessica snapped at him. "You will get caught."

"I doubt it." Victor smiled. He looked at his watch. Sell time was approaching. "Oh, we have a full house today," he said laughing. "All those other jewels are being bought quickly. My overseas account is getting larger by the minute."

Victor looked over at Sean.

"Go put her in front of the camera. Her time is coming soon."

Sean took Jessica's arm and escorted her to the spot in middle of the cameras and spotlights. She yanked her arm away from Sean. Sean took her hair and pulled it more over her shoulders. He brushed his fingers across her cheek. Immediately Jessica raised her hand and slapped Sean across the face. Shock rattled through him as he was not expecting that, however it was perfect for those who were watching. Victor let out a hearty laugh.

"You led me on," Jessica said. "I trusted you."

"One thing you need to learn, Jess, never trust the bad guy," Sean replied as he touched his stinging cheek. He gave her a quick wink then backed away.

Sean was pleased at the way Jessica was acting. Victor put on his headset and pressed a button and began speaking. He announced that the bids were now closed and very shortly would be the final bid for the evening.

Sean put his hands in his pocket and carefully pushed the S.O.S. button on the side of his phone, sending a coded backup message to his fellow agents. He knew his team wasn't too far away because they were tracking him already. But when would they show up? He wasn't quite sure.

"Oh, isn't it lovely?" Victor gazed at the necklace around Jessica's neck.

All Sean could see was Jessica's beauty.

"Yes, she is," Sean replied.

"You can't fool me, Sean," Victor laughed. "You want the girl. Well, if you want her, you are going to need to bid for her like everyone else."

Victor pressed the button on his headset and spoke.

"The bidding for the Midnight Star and its beautiful model begins now. Starting bid Three Million." Victor's face beamed with greed as his laptop began sounding notifications in rapid succession.

Sean heard the dings on the laptop as bids were being placed. His heart hammered against his ribs as any moment, things were going to change. Jessica's face grew pale and she shot a scared look towards Sean.

Sean felt his phone vibrate two times in his pocket. That was his notification that backup had arrived.

"Enough Victor," Sean yelled out. "Your time has run out. I've already contacted the police. They know you have the diamond."

As soon as Sean mentioned *police* all the men outside of their room began scrambling and shutting down the black market site. Laptops were being thrown into bags and people were scattering like the place was going to blow up. Victor frantically looked around.

"Sean, what are you doing?" Victor asked, reaching for his belt buckle.

Immediately, Sean flipped the metal table over and pulled Jessica down with him behind the table. As quick as he could he reached up Jessica's dress and pulled out the gun, causing Jessica to gasp in surprise. Sean peaked over the top of the table pointing his gun at Victor. Sean had expected Victor to have a gun, but was surprised to see that it was the small 4 shot pistol from his belt buckle.

"I thought you said that wasn't a real gun," Sean quipped.

"Oh, it's real, alright." Victor laughed pulling the hammer back. "They just never questioned. Perks of working the Black Market."

"Your Black Market days are finished, Victor. You are under arrest."

"You and what army, Sean. Last I checked, you're just one man."

"Actually, I'm much more than you know. Agent Turpin, FBI. Drop your weapon."

"No-no, you drop your gun, Sean, you have no backup," Victor walked a little closer keeping the gun on Sean.

With Sean's free hand that was behind the table he was fumbling up Jessica's dress, trying to reach for the holster that was around her leg. With his eyes locked on Victor's, and Jessica slapping his arm, it was extremely difficult to grasp what he was reaching for.

"So, you think you are FBI?" Victor laughed. "What a liar you are. Stand up you fool."

Sean, with his gun still pointed towards Victor, slowly stood up. He didn't want to take a bullet, but if it meant keeping Jessica safe, he would.

"You aren't going to win this one, Victor," Sean told him. "My team will be here soon."

"I'm going to take the girl and go now," Victor said as he maneuvered to the side of the table.

"Over my dead body," Sean replied.

****

Jessica's heart was beating so fast she thought for sure she would die of a heart attack. There was no way she was going with Victor. Locked in a staring war, Victor and Sean kept their guns pointed at each other. Victor moved stealthily, like a panther after its prey, nearing the overturned table where she was. Adrenaline kicked in shooting energy through her body like she'd never experienced before. She couldn't just stay still and let someone take her-or kill her. She grasped two of the table legs. Just as Victor stepped close enough, and she pushed the table with all her might. The piece of furniture slammed into Victor, knocking him off guard. He stumbled back.

At that moment, Sean leaped onto Victor. The second their bodies connected, the fast motion had Sean in control as the two men tumbled to the ground. Both guns clattered to the floor. Victor immediately threw a punch, hitting Sean in the jaw. Her hero wasn't fazed, and he struck back. The blow Sean delivered to Victor snapped his head to the side. Unfortunately, Victor was a large man and probably use to this kind of treatment. Struggling, the two continued hitting each other, and yet, Sean was still on top and in control. However, eventually someone was going to weaken, and she didn't want it to be Sean.

Victor kept reaching for his gun, but Sean's hit would jerk him away. Jessica stood on shaky legs. She assessed the scene, not quite knowing what to do. All she knew was that she needed to somehow kick the guns away from Victor's reach.

Victor landed a punch on Sean's jaw and rolled over, grabbing Jessica by the ankle, and pulled her down. His hand reached for Sean's gun just as Sean grasped Victor's pistol. Victor stood up and pulled Jessica to her feet. He had blood trickling from his nose and lip. His steely arm wrapped around her neck in a choke hold as he pointed the gun at Sean.

She struggled to pull his arm away, gradually losing her breath, but it was impossible. Victor would not budge.

"Nice try," Victor laughed. He began backing up with Jessica in his arms towards the door. "You know, I never really wanted the girl. With the money from this diamond alone, I can have a whole harem of women." Victor reached up and yanked the necklace from Jessica's neck.

Jessica yelped. She'd seen that done many times in the movies, but she never knew it would actually hurt as bad as it did. It probably left a good burn mark or cut on the back of her neck.

The corners of Sean's lips rose as a smile slowly covered his face.

"You really haven't figured it out yet?" Sean asked coyly keeping the pistol pointed at Victor.

"Quit trying to distract me," Victor growled. "I should just kill you both now."

"Go ahead," Sean urged on. "Do it."

"No, Sean," Jessica sobbed. "What are you doing? Don't say that!"

Victor steadily aimed the gun at Sean's head. Jessica's head swam with dizziness, yet she had to stay strong to help him. Fainting would only bring on her death quicker.

"Do it, Victor!" Sean demanded. "Pull the trigger!"

Jessica closed her eyes tightly as Victor squeezed the trigger. *Click.*

No shot rang out. Jessica opened her eyes and gasped. Victor's face was wrinkled with confusion as he pulled the trigger again. *Click.* Nothing. He tried a few more times, but the click of the empty chamber only made him more upset.

Victor's face quickly drained of color.

"You know, for a thief, Victor, I would have thought you'd know the difference between a loaded gun and an empty one." Sean laughed. "In fact, I bet even Jessica could tell you that."

Victor shook his head in disbelief and threw the gun against the wall in frustration.

"Hmmm," Sean said, brandishing Victor's pistol with a smile, "I wonder if yours is loaded?"

"Sean, how did you get a gun in here anyway? They patted you down," Victor asked as he backed closer to the door, the Midnight Star still grasped tightly in his hands.

"Don't touch the merchandise," Sean replied, winking at Jessica.

****

Suddenly, Victor shoved Jessica. She stumbled towards Sean. Victor turned quickly, throwing the door open to make his escape. Jessica fell into Sean's arms, but he quickly pulled her to the side. He stooped down and picked up his own gun while keeping the other gun pointed at Victor. With both guns in hand, he took off after him. Sean chased Victor across the now empty and abandoned warehouse floor. Reaching the entrance, Victor flung the door open. As he stepped out into the crisp nighttime air, spotlights shone on him and the sound of 20 or more rifles being cocked echoed across the parking lot. All of them were pointed directly at Victor. He stopped in his tracks.

"Victor McGunther," an FBI Agent announced over the speaker. "Put your hands in the air. You are under arrest for the theft of the Midnight Star among other robberies, and for kidnapping."

"It's over, Victor. Drop to your knees," Sean said standing behind him.

Victor dropped to his knees. Sean put the smaller pistol in his pocket and grabbed the diamond from Victor's hand. As Sean stepped back, five officers came and surrounded Victor.

Sean lowered his gun and handed the diamond to another FBI Agent and they took it away. Sean turned to look behind him and saw Jessica walking slowly towards him. He quickly jogged over to her and she slid into his arms just as her legs gave out, pulling him down to the cool floor with her.

"H-he could have shot you." Jessica had tears running down her cheeks leaving smeared mascara trails.

"Not without this," Sean said as he reached up her dress and moved his hand slowly up her leg. He heard her suck in a breath at his touch. He stopped at her thigh and he unbuckled the gun holster and pulled it off. He took out the loaded magazine that was tucked inside the holster and clicked it into his gun. "I didn't put the magazine in the gun because I didn't want you to accidently shoot yourself."

Jessica pushed her head into his shoulder and began sobbing. Sean wrapped his arms around her and pulled her close. He kissed the top of her head.

"You are safe now," he whispered.

NINETEEN

Jessica stood at her window at Winslow Bank helping a customer. It had been a month since her kidnapping. Victor was behind bars as well as Bruce, Connie and Jack. She hadn't seen Sean since the night Victor was arrested and she had been taken back to her house.

After days of crying over a broken heart, she went back to work, taking the advice of Connie and wearing better fitting clothes and straightening her hair more. She even went and purchased some contacts and realized it wasn't as bad as she thought sticking her fingers in her eyes to put the contacts in.

Jessica was very thankful that her boss didn't fire her for being MIA for a couple of weeks. Life was slowly going back to the way things were before, with the exception of Trent Hawkins.

"Jessica," Trent whispered over the wall to her in-between customers. "Do you want to go for drinks after work?"

Ever since Jessica returned back to work, Trent was now constantly around her. He was doing his best to flirt with her and trying to get her to go out with him. After being with Sean for that week, she had no desire to be with anyone else, at least not yet.

"Sorry, Trent," Jessica whispered. "I've been invited to my parents' home for dinner. Thank you, though." Jessica smiled the best she could. It was nearing closing time and she did not want to go anywhere with him.

"Another time," Trent replied as he went back to helping the next customer.

Jessica sighed. After seven years of trying to get Trent to notice her, she couldn't care less now. Her heart still ached for only one man. She focused on her computer screen and was closing out of certain screens to prepare for closing when a wad of hundred dollar bills and a driver's license and bank card was pushed in front of her.

"I'd like to make a deposit." A deep voice said.

Jessica's eyes jumped to the driver's license. The name and picture was of none other than Sean Turpin. Her eyes shot up to meet his. Her heart rate increased as she gazed upon the man that she couldn't get out of her mind for the past month. He wore a light blue dress shirt and a black tie matching his black pants. His beard was trimmed shorter. She couldn't help but suck in a breath at how handsome he was.

"Hey, Jess," he said with a smile.

"S-Sean," she stammered. "Where have you been?"

"Working," he said. "I had to debrief and round up the other three. Work has kept me very busy."

"You couldn't call me?" Jessica could feel tears starting to form in her eyes.

"No, honey, I couldn't," Sean said as he reached across and took her hand. "Can I see you after work?"

Jessica's hands began to tremble and then she nodded.

"Alright," she whispered. She licked her lips then asked, "Do you want this in checking or savings?"

"Savings." He gave her a wink and she smiled and proceeded with the transaction.

Jessica wasn't sure why he came back to see her. In her heart she carried a small amount of hope. His scent lingered at her work station after he disappeared outside. Now she couldn't focus. Why did he want to see her?

"Who was that?" Charlene asked her as they finished up their drawer counts.

"Umm," Jessica wasn't quite sure how to answer that. "He's with the FBI."

"FBI?" Charlene's eyes went big. "He is gorgeous. I think he likes you."

Jessica shrugged her shoulders. The way he took off a month ago, she had to question that thought.

At 6:30 p.m., Jessica walked outside of the bank with Charlene. Leaning against his silver Camaro was Sean. He stood up straighter as they drew nearer. In his hand was a red rose. Charlene gave her a little elbow nudge with a smile and turned and left Jessica standing in front of Sean.

"Hi," Jessica started. She was trying her hardest to not make a huge scene by throwing her arms around him or slapping his face.

"How have you been?" Sean asked handing her the rose. "I've missed you."

Jessica closed the space in between them. She brought the rose to her nose and breathed in its fragrance.

"I still have a job," she said with a smile.

"I'm pleased to know that."

"I thought you wouldn't come back." Jessica could feel the lump in her throat starting to get larger. She really didn't want to cry.

Sean reached out to her and took her hands and pulled her closer to him. He put his arms around her waist and nuzzled his face against hers. His short, well-groomed beard tickled her cheek.

"Nothing will keep me away from you ever again," he whispered. "Jess, I love you."

Jessica moved her gaze to his dark brown eyes.

"Do you really?" She asked. "I've wrestled in my mind trying to figure out if you are a good guy or a bad guy."

"It's hard living a double life," Sean said as he brushed his lips across hers. "But I'm done doing that now. I only want to live a life with you in it."

Jessica's body was tingling with emotion overload. She slid the palms of her hands up his chest and stopped at his shoulders.

"I was wondering," Jessica asked as she met his lips briefly again. "Would you like to come back to my place for a Peanut Butter and Jelly sandwich?"

Sean smiled and placed his lips fully on top of hers and deepened their kiss.

"I love you, Jess," he whispered. "I'll go with you anywhere."

"I love you so much," Jessica sighed, touching her fingers to his lips.

This was much better than a romance novel and she couldn't wait to have more adventures with him. As his lips touched hers again, she knew life with Sean was going to be full of excitement.

THE END

Author Stacey Haynes' Bio

Stacey Haynes has always enjoyed reading and writing romance stories beginning with her first story in 6th grade. Her dream had always been to have one of her books published. Stacey currently has two books that she has co-authored with her sister, Marie Higgins, and also has another published work, a poem about her most disliked food, Peas!

She won her first writing contest when she and her sister, Marie, entered their story *The Magic of a Billionaire* into an online writing contest on www.ajoara.com – and their story won 1st place!

She considers herself a hopeless romantic and tries to find the best in others. She loves to write and do things with her family in her spare time to relax after a hard day at work.

Stacey lives in Utah, with her wonderful husband and three adorable children. She hopes to have more books published in her lifetime. You can follow her adventures on Facebook at http://www.facebook.com/StaceyHaynes and https://www.facebook.com/Stacey-Haynes-Author-110345070332647

Other books by Stacey Haynes that can be found on Amazon and Kindle Unlimited and paperback:

The Magic of a Billionaire by Marie Higgins and Stacey Haynes https://www.amazon.com/Magic-Billionaire-Tycoons-Book-ebook/dp/B07VZT8S6Y
The Billionaire's Setup by Marie Higgins and Stacey Haynes - https://www.amazon.com/Billionaires-Setup-Tycoons-Book-10-ebook/dp/B07Y9DMRHY

Made in the USA
Middletown, DE
24 March 2023